DISCOVERED PROMISES

DISCOVERED PROMISES

THE DISCOVERED TRUTH SERIES ROMANTIC SUSPENSE
BOOK SIXTEEN

JULIE BAWDEN DAVIS

Cover by Judy Bullard (customebookcovers.com)

Book design by Julie Bawden-Davis

Palm logo design by Kayla Curry

Roses are Red logo design by Kyle Kane

ISBN 13: 978-1-955265-38-6

ISBN 10: 1-955265-38-0

Distributed by Roses Are Red Publishing

rosesareredpublishing.com

❀ Created with Vellum

ACKNOWLEDGMENTS

As they say, it takes a village. Here's my village. I'm supremely grateful to each of these fabulous people!

ARC Reading Gems
Julie Schlueter
Tara Bradley
Susa Fraccaroli
Kery Bailey
Trish Darrenkamp
Marilyn Smith
Lisa Starkey
Beth Helm
Chelle Young
Jacquelyn Gray
Penny McCulloch
Ellen White
Heather Wamboldt
MelK
Monte Bawden
Amber Mancebo

Pros
Judy Bullard, cover design
Kyle Kane, logo design
Sabrina Wildermuth, design consultation
Jeremy Davis, technical support

To those in need of a sense of home.

PROLOGUE - MAY 2008

"The land belongs to our people, but you need to prove it."
Skip's mother's voice was low, raspy.

Skip held her hand and leaned in closer. This was the first
time he'd heard of land. "What do you mean, Mom?"

She ran her tongue across her lips. "The land they stole
from us. You need to get it back for the Sioux people."

Skip picked up the cup of water on the bedside table and
put his hand behind his mother's head. He helped her lean
toward the cup. She took several sips, then lay back on her
pillow. The bedside clock ticked softly. He thought she had
started to doze off from the morphine he'd just given her, but
she turned to him then, her eyes bright like they used to be.

"In my chest in the spare bedroom, there are papers," she
said. "Promise me you'll do this. For our people."

Skip studied his mother, her regal chin stubbornly fixed,
her long, black hair spun with silver in a braid beside her on
the bed.

"Does Pop know about the land?"

His mother turned her gaze back toward the ceiling. "He
said to let it go. That we'd only bring trouble to our door."

"Why didn't you tell me before?"

His mother sighed and her eyes fluttered closed. "Because it wasn't time before." Her breathing slowed, and in moments she was asleep.

Skip gently extricated his hand from her grasp and left his mother's room. As he walked down the hallway, the familiar creak of the floorboards steadied him. He leaned for a moment in the open doorway of the spare room to gather his thoughts. He'd been by his mother's side since the vigil had begun two months before, when the doctors had given her a month to live. Each day that they got closer to the end, Skip's heart felt heavier, his spirit more anguished.

In the bedroom, he went to the wooden chest against the wall and began checking drawers. Most were empty, but a few held odds and ends like spare buttons and colorful spools of thread. He was about to give up looking when he pulled open a drawer and found an old manila envelope, the paper aged, the edges frayed. He picked it up and turned it over and began unwinding the string that held it closed.

1

PRESENT DAY

Skip Moore finished up his flight log and did a final check of his Cessna before heading out of the airport for the night. It was early May and not hurricane season yet here in Acapulco but it would be soon. He made double sure the plane was secure after he tied it down.

It had been a long week flying, and he was ready to kick back and drink a beer—or three. Hoisting his bag onto one shoulder, he headed toward his car. He had walked only a few paces before someone came running across the tarmac toward him. He stopped, soon seeing it was a woman. She wore a black sweatshirt with a hood and a long, flowing dark skirt. "You have to help me," she said, stopping a few feet from him, out of breath, striking hazel eyes wide. She had long, auburn hair and a beauty mark high on one cheek.

"What's the problem?" He glanced around and didn't see anyone else. "If you're in trouble, you should call the police." He repositioned his bag.

Terror raced across her face, and she shook her head. "Not the police."

Just what he didn't need—to be found with a fugitive. "Are you wanted by the police?"

"Please, can we take your plane? I'll pay you. I just need it to be now."

"Where?" He asked the question, with no intention of getting involved.

"Anywhere," she begged.

"I can't just take you anywhere. Pilots need a manifest, a destination." He started to walk away.

The woman suddenly pulled a gun out of her pocket and aimed it at his chest. "Stop where you are, or I'll pull the trigger. Get the plane ready for takeoff. Now!"

Skip slipped his bag from his shoulder and let it drop to the ground. "Whoa, hold on. I'm willing to hear what you have to say. Put the gun away and we can talk about this. I'm a good listener." He thought about rushing her and grabbing the weapon, but decided to let things play out.

"I'll put the gun down when we're in the air headed away from here." She took several steps back and quickly glanced around, then refocused on him.

"Running usually isn't the answer," said Skip. "Just let me help you figure this out."

She let out a harsh laugh. "I guarantee you can't help me figure this out." She gestured to his plane with her gun. "Go back and get us out of here. If you don't, I can't be responsible for you getting caught in the crossfire."

Just then Skip noticed a car speeding down the road coming toward them. Unusual for this time of night, and it wasn't a police car.

The woman looked back and shrieked, "Please."

Skip picked up his bag, mad as hell at her for getting him involved. "C'mon."

They raced to the plane, and he quickly untied it. "Get in," he yelled. As he turned on the engine, the car reached the runway. He began making his way down the tarmac.

"Fly already," the woman yelled.

That's not the way it works, Skip thought, seeing now as he taxied that the car had stopped and two men had exited the vehicle and were running after them. Both held guns. As he lifted off the runway, the radio crackled and he heard a voice. Most likely the airport watch commander wanting to know why he was taking off at a prohibited time. So much for getting out of there undetected. He checked his coordinates. They were heading southeast.

He glanced over at the woman, who gripped the gun in her lap with both hands and looked out the window at the scene below.

"We're safe," he said finally. "Put the safety on that thing."

She glanced at him, distrust in her eyes.

"The gun goes off and shoots me, it's all over. You're going to fall through the sky like a wounded bird."

She set the safety and placed the gun back on her lap.

"I refueled when I stopped for the night but I can't go on indefinitely," he said. "Do you have a plan?"

She let go of the gun long enough to wipe stray hairs from her cheek, then said, "How far can you go?"

"The direction we're going, I can get as far as Panama. If you're trying to get to the States, the best I could do—and it would be a maybe—is fly into Laredo, Texas."

"Not the US," she said. "Fly into Panama."

"Then what?" asked Skip as he set the course.

"You let me off, and I go on my way. As promised, I'll pay you for your trouble."

"I don't want dirty money."

"It's my money," she said, almost under her breath. "I earned it." She leaned her head back on the seat.

Skip looked over at her face in the dim light of the plane's control panel. It was lined with fatigue, dark circles under her eyes. "There are some water bottles in the back, if you want."

She opened her eyes and reached behind him, retrieving two bottles, handing one to him and opening another for herself. He watched out of the corner of his eye as she took a long drink, nearly downing half the bottle at once.

"We've got about three hours to Panama," he said.

She nodded slightly, then began loosening the edge of the water bottle label with her forefinger. "I know I could have gotten you killed. I just didn't know what else to do."

"How about you repay me by telling me what's going on?" said Skip. "Who is after you? I sure as hell hope you haven't gotten me involved with a cartel."

"It's best you don't know."

Skip laughed. "Too late for that. I've had a gun waved at me, people chasing after my plane, and now I'm heading to an airport that isn't expecting us. I deserve an answer. But first, I'm Skip. You are?"

"Liliana," she said softly.

"Okay, now who or what has you running, Liliana?"

"You wouldn't believe me if I told you."

"Try me."

She looked out the window into the dark night. "My father."

2

At the look of astonishment on Skip's face, she said, "I told you that you wouldn't believe me."

"You're right, I don't believe you," he said.

Liliana threw up her hands and slapped them down on her lap. "Okay, that was a cartel, but they're the least of my worries."

Skip didn't know this woman. She seemed like a con. Who knew what she had in mind. He checked the fuel level, then turned on his radio. He needed to let the airport know he would be coming in.

"You're not saying anything," she said after a few minutes of silence.

Skip looked straight ahead. "You seem caught up in something I don't want to be a part of. When we get to Panama, you can pay me for my aggravation and fuel, then we part ways." It seemed to Skip she was in way over her head. All he knew was this woman meant nothing but trouble.

Liliana watched as Skip radioed into the airport. She understood enough Spanish to know they weren't happy with him making an unexpected landing. She gazed out into the dark night and thought how quiet and peaceful it was up here flying above the clouds. It felt comforting, which was something she hadn't experienced in a long time.

"How long have you been flying?" she asked.

Skip didn't answer at first. Instead, he checked the gauges and mumbled something about the weather. "All my life. My pop was a farmer in North Dakota, so he used Cessnas for fertilizing crops. He taught me."

"Is your father not farming anymore?"

Skip shook his head "He sold the farm a couple years ago and moved to a retirement community in Florida with my stepmother."

"And your mother?"

"What's with all the questions?"

"I'm just making conversation," said Liliana. "Never mind." She closed her eyes. If he wasn't up for conversation, she might as well get some rest. Once they touched down, she'd be running again.

After a while, Skip saw that Liliana was sleeping. She didn't stir, face even prettier when she was calm. He looked at her for a minute, curves of thick hair hugging her shoulders. Even in a black hoodie, he could tell she was shapely.

Skip checked his watch, past midnight. He took a deep breath, amazed to think he was carting this stranger, although by force, to an entirely different country. He puffed out his cheeks and blew a stream of air from his lips. At least being in command of the Cessna calmed him. Though night flying always carried a degree of risk with visibility a factor, he enjoyed it for the peace it brought.

"One day, the farm will be yours," said Skip's father.

It was a late summer day, and they stood on the edge of one of their vast oat fields. Skip was fourteen, a head taller than his father already, and had just finished helping him and several of their farmhands glean the fields.

"You're quiet," said his father, who finished with his habit of picking his teeth with a piece of straw and tossed it back onto the field.

Skip didn't have the courage to tell him what he thought of taking over the farm one day. "Just hungry, is all," he said.

"Let's go see what your mother cooked up for supper." His father turned and headed back toward the farmhouse.

Just then, Skip heard a distinctive rumble. He stopped and looked to the east as a plane came out of the clouds and flew overhead toward the local airport. He felt an excited rush in his chest as the aircraft jetted through the sky. How could he tell his pop that he wanted to be in the cockpit—not behind a tractor?

When they were near the airport, Liliana stirred and opened her eyes. She stretched her neck and took a sip of water. "I'm sorry about all of this," she said quietly. "The last thing I wanted to do was put you in harm's way. But I was out of options."

Skip shrugged. "As a private pilot, I've been in plenty of predicaments."

"I'm sure you have some stories to tell." She opened her backpack and took out her wallet. "How much would be fair for tonight?"

Skip thought for a moment. "Five hundred will cover it."

Liliana took out six hundred and handed the bills to him. He stuffed them into his shirt pocket, then picked up his radio and confirmed their pending arrival. Landing in unfamiliar airports was not something he enjoyed. Though arriving in the middle of night meant there was less air traffic, he didn't know what to expect in terms of terrain and runway conditions, and that bothered him.

Despite his qualms, ten minutes later they were taxiing down the runway. He had arranged to park in the hangar for the rest of the night.

After Skip secured the plane, he and Liliana headed to the small terminal. Stepping through the back door, they left the humid night behind and were greeted by a rush of cool, refreshing air. Skip looked around to see the lights were low. A smattering of travelers sat around waiting, but otherwise things were quiet. He stopped and turned to Liliana. "Stay safe," he said.

She hesitated. "Where are you staying?"

"I'm going to get some shut-eye here in the terminal, then head out first thing."

"Oh, well, thank you again." She held out her hand, which Skip took in his. She had a strong grip, though her skin was smooth and soft.

"Maybe there is someone on duty who can suggest a nearby hotel," he said, her hand still in his as he wondered why he was so concerned about someone who had taken him hostage. They stood that way for a moment until Skip cleared his throat.

Liliana responded by removing her hand from his and adjusting her backpack on her shoulder. "That's a good idea. I'll ask someone. Have a good night."

As Skip watched Liliana walk away, he had to admit, the possibility of what could happen to her once she was on her own gave him a sinking feeling.

3

Skip sat down and checked his cellphone. An email from his stepmother.

I tried calling but it went straight to voicemail, so I'm hoping this email gets to you. Your dad had a fall last night and is in the hospital. Please call me as soon as possible. Helen

His heart doing a tap dance in his chest, Skip dialed his stepmother's number and waited while it rang.

"Skip, thank goodness." Her voice was hushed.

"How is he?"

"Hold on. I'm going into the hallway."

A door opened and closed, then she spoke, her voice louder now. "At first, we thought he'd be okay. He got up right after falling and went to sit in his armchair to get his bearings. But when I got back from getting him some water, I found him slumped over. I immediately called 911."

"And now?"

"He says his head hurts, so they're doing some tests. I know you're busy, but do you think you could come? The doctors say it could be something minor, but if it's more serious, I'd feel better if you were here."

"Of course," said Skip. "I'm in Panama, so closer than I would be if I was home. The airport will allow me to take off in about three hours, and it'll take me another three or so to get to Sarasota."

"Oh, good. I know he'll be happy to see you."

"I'll be there as soon as I can."

He closed his phone and his eyes locked on the empty seat across the aisle as he recalled the last time he'd seen his father. It had been months. At the time, he had seemed his old self. While Skip knew he always missed his mother and never ceased loving her, Helen was a good, kind woman who helped ease his father's loneliness and looked after him. Skip was grateful for that.

"Do you know why we named you Skip?"

Skip was ten at the time, and he and his mother were in the garden weeding the flowerbed.

She wore her long, black hair in a pigtail. An old cotton dress swept around her ankles as she moved.

"No, why?"

She bent down and stabbed a trowel into the earth, then sat back on her haunches. "I wanted to give you a traditional Sioux name but your father and I didn't want things to be difficult for you." She looked up at the sky as she spoke. "Rather than give you a name that you might want to change, we chose Skip."

He looked up at the cloud formation his mother was staring at. "But why Skip?"

She smiled as a crow flew overhead. "Because from the moment you were born, I knew you would make a difference. When you throw a stone along the water's surface, it skips, creating waves that ripple in every direction."

Skip sighed at the memory, the familiar ache at missing his mother washing through him. So often in his life, he longed for her wise counsel. That was yet another reason he loved flying. Up in the quiet of the clouds, time suspended, he felt close to her.

Liliana stood in the airport bathroom, wondering what her next move should be. She had run through multiple scenarios and none of them seemed viable or even possible. Finally, she decided her only option was to get lost in the Panamanian countryside. She'd lie low until daybreak, then get a ride to El Valle. She had heard it was beautiful there, and most importantly, remote.

A couple of hours later, Liliana got some hot tea from a kiosk and a tortilla changa, which she ate quickly. As she scarfed the food down, she tried to remember when she last ate. Was it yesterday at breakfast? The days were blurring together, as they had been for the last six months. She was about to order another tortilla when her phone buzzed. She checked the screen and her heart sank. Her handler, and exactly what she was afraid of.

We have your exact location and we're coming to get you. Stay put.

Liliana felt like screaming. How could she do what the FBI wanted? The consequences of complying were too extreme. Now they were already coming for her. Her appetite lost, she abandoned the idea of eating another tortilla and sat down, clasping the tea in her lap. How long did she have, she wondered?

After getting some breakfast and filling a thermos with coffee, Skip went out into the muggy early morning and prepared his plane for takeoff. Then he got in and started the engine, awaiting word he could begin taxiing. Radar showed storms in the distance, and he wanted to get up above them before there was a real problem. Just when he was given the order to proceed, the passenger door flew open and Liliana jumped in.

"No," he started.

"Please. I can't stay here." The terror in her eyes was apparent. "They've found me."

Skip checked around quickly. "They're here now?"

"They will be soon. Please take me somewhere else. Not back to Acapulco. I'll double what I paid you."

The tower then repeated that he was cleared to take the runway.

"I'll go anywhere," she added.

Skip clenched his teeth and steered the plane onto the tarmac. "We're going to Florida."

"I told you I can't go to the States," she cried.

"If you don't want to go, now is the time to get out."

When Liliana didn't answer, Skip started taxiing.

4

Skip should have left Liliana on the tarmac, but he'd caused enough commotion at the airport. Besides, he'd never seen that much fear on anyone in his life.

"I know this is getting to be a habit. Get me out of here, and you'll never see me again. I'm truly sorry," said Liliana after a few minutes of silence.

"For waving a gun at me, forcing me to fly to Panama, or saying you were leaving and jumping back onto my plane?"

She put her head in her hands and murmured, "All of it. I've been forced into a corner. The only thing I can do is try and outrun them."

Skip had the urge to let her know how much he regretted running into her but kept quiet. Instead, he checked his gauges. He had refueled at the airport, so he would have plenty of gas to get to Sarasota.

"What could be so important to drag you to Florida this minute?" Liliana frowned at him. "I'll triple my offer if you take me to another country." She was quiet for a moment. "Okay, how much do you want?"

"My father has been hospitalized. I have to get there."

Liliana felt terrible to be imposing on the challenges of Skip's personal life. She sighed and ran through her options. She needed to let this guy get on with his life while she figured out hers. The only viable option she could think of was getting ahold of fake identification papers, then somehow blending into the Florida landscape. But for how long? They'd find her eventually.

She gazed out the window and saw blue water in the distance. "Is that the Caribbean up ahead?"

"Yes," said Skip as the air suddenly became choppy, bumping the plane. Liliana held onto the edge of her seat, heart pounding. "Are we going to be okay?"

"It will be smoother once we're over water. When you see land in a couple of hours, that'll be Cuba. Right before that will be the Caymans."

"Does flying ever scare you?" She turned toward him.

Skip shook his head. "I figure if I meet my end when flying, then that's the way I'm supposed to go."

"Just like that?"

Skip shrugged. "There would be much worse ways to go."

He was right about that, thought Liliana. The thought of plunging through the sky would be preferable to what they'd do to her for her betrayal.

When they were a few minutes out from landing in Sarasota, Liliana asked, "You wouldn't happen to know anyone who could get me some fake papers?"

"As a matter of fact, I do."

Liliana was surprised. "You do?"

"A buddy of mine from another time, let's just say. I'll hook you up when we land."

After they were on the ground again and Skip had powered down the plane, he scrawled a name and number onto a scrap of paper and handed it to her. Then he turned and walked toward the terminal, leaving her standing in the hangar.

Liliana watched him go, then checked out the paper he had given her. It read Carlos Rincon and had a Florida phone number. She called and waited.

A voice answered after several rings, *"Hola."*

"Skip gave me your number," she said. "I need some paperwork."

"Skip who?"

"He didn't tell me his last name. Just that you could hook me up."

"I'm going to need more than that *chica*. Let me talk to him."

"I can't. He just left."

"How do you know him?" asked the man, his voice suspicious.

"He flew me in from Panama just now, and he has a personal matter to attend to. We met in Mexico."

"Where in Mexico?"

"Acapulco."

The man paused for a few moments. "I happen to have an opening this afternoon, if you can get here quickly."

Liliana had the driver drop her off a block away from her destination. She lifted the hair from the back of her neck, sticky with sweat from the humidity, and draped it over one shoulder. Then she walked toward a towering apartment building surrounded by bright-green lawn, bird of paradise flanking the main walkway. After climbing the stairs to the third floor, she stopped at number 303 and knocked.

"*Quien es?*"

"I called earlier." She waited on the doorstep, sensing someone checking her out through the peephole.

The door opened and there stood a man in board shorts, a blue tank top stretched over his solid chest. A goatee covering his chin matched heavy brows and wavy black hair. He stepped back, dark eyes wary, and motioned for her to come in.

Liliana entered a heavily air-conditioned living room with loft ceilings. Across the apartment was a spacious kitchen and a sliding glass door leading out onto a balcony.

"Have a seat." He pointed to a leather couch. "You want the works, right?" He picked a metal box off a shelf and put it on the table, opening it with a key from his key chain.

"Yes. How soon can I get them?"

"About an hour, maybe less." He took out a camera. "Stand against the wall, over there."

She did as he asked.

"You might want to smile," he suggested. "Looks more natural."

Liliana gave a fake smile as he took the photo.

"Have you known Skip long?" she asked.

He pursed his lips for a second, then grinned. "He didn't tell you?"

"Only that he knows you from a former life."

"So that's what he's saying." His eyes crinkled at the corners.

Liliana waited, but Carlos didn't elaborate further. She wondered what Skip was doing now.

5

Skip stopped the rental car in front of his father's home and let out a breath he didn't realize he was holding in. He peered at the one-story house, sand-colored against a blue sky studded with clouds. He got out of the car, greeted by the sound of rustling palm trees. Crotons lined the path to the front porch where a fountain trickled. A quick knock on the door, and it swung open.

"Thank you for getting here so quickly," said Helen. Her perfume, a sweet fragrance, reached him first.

He hugged her and walked into the house, decorated in his stepmother's signature white. White carpeting, white couch, and white drapes matched the equally snowy toy poodle that came scampering up to sniff his pant leg. Skip reached down and ruffled the dog's head. "Hey, Mr. Skittles." Then he stood and squared his shoulders. "How's Pop doing?"

"Better. They're conducting a bunch of testing on him now. I figured you could get settled, then we can go over once he's back in his room."

Skip nodded. "I appreciate it. I could really use a shower."

Helen turned and began walking down a hallway. She opened the door to the guest room, decorated in pale green and white. It had a window overlooking a large patio lined with colorful flowerbeds.

"There are towels in the bathroom," she said. "I'll be on the lanai."

A half-hour later, Skip was refreshed and had changed into jeans and a T-shirt. He walked down the hallway and past the expansive kitchen. Through a sliding glass door, he saw Helen sitting in a rattan chair looking at her phone. She had a slight frame—barely a hundred pounds, he imagined. Her hair, dyed a shade of dirty-blonde, was short and neat, bangs cut across her forehead. When he pulled the screen door open, she glanced up.

"I poured you a glass of lemonade." She pointed to a tall glass on the table next to her.

Skip went over and sat down and took a long drink. He hadn't realized how thirsty he was until now. "That hit the spot. Thank you."

Helen glanced again at her phone. "The nurse texted to say they'll be done with his MRI in a few minutes. The hospital is just down the street."

Skip glanced around the lanai, noting several bright-green hanging ferns and vivid red anthuriums.

"Your father's handiwork. When we left the farm, he swore he was done planting. But within a few months, the green bug hit, so he started growing ferns and such."

"It's nice," said Skip.

Helen sighed. "Before we go, I want to prepare you. Your father has lost some weight."

Skip sat up.

"I tried to convince him to check in with you and tell you what was happening, but he refused."

Skip's heart thudded uncomfortably in his chest. "What *is* happening with him?"

"The weight loss started about a month ago. At first they thought maybe he'd eaten something that gave him a parasite. But your father isn't into sushi and that sort of thing, so they ruled it out after some testing. They also checked for malaria, since there are mosquitoes here and there have been more outbreaks. But all of that brought up nothing."

Skip didn't want to ask, but he did. "What about cancer?"

"They've been checking for that as well, but still nothing. He was feeling somewhat better the last couple of weeks, so we were getting hopeful, but then he had the dizzy spell yesterday and fell."

"What now?"

"They are going to keep doing testing in hopes that they find something. He might be upset that I called you, but I felt you should know."

Skip sat back in the chair. "I appreciate that."

Her phone flashed, and she picked it up. "They said we can see him now."

Skip started to get up, but she held up her hand. "There's one more thing."

He sat back and waited.

"A few weeks ago, someone came to visit him. A woman. I'm not sure who she was or what she said to him."

"He didn't tell you what she wanted?"

Helen shook her head. "They came out here to the lanai, and I could tell that your dad wanted privacy, so I stayed in the living room. I figured he'd fill me in when she left, but he didn't. When I asked, he said not to worry about it. You know your father. When he clams up about something, there's no point in asking."

"Had you seen the woman before? Maybe she's from the Dakota land management board he was involved in."

"I've met many of the people your dad dealt with over the last few years. She wasn't one of them."

"How old was she?"

"I'd say thirty something. Maybe Native American. I'm sorry I don't know more, but it seemed significant." She stood. "We better go. Your father is going to wonder where I am."

The late afternoon sun blazed as they made their way to the hospital. As Helen drove, Skip couldn't stop thinking about the mystery woman. It wasn't like his father to keep secrets.

"Lift the throttle when you see the top of the corn—the tassels," said his father as they made their way across the back acres of land near the farm. Skip was fifteen, and it was his first flight to fertilize the fields.

"Now," said his father.

Skip pulled up on the throttle and felt the plane's engine shift into a steady hum.

"Now we're going to unload the spray," said his father. "Go ahead and press the button and continue at the same speed, like I showed you."

Skip did as his father told him, hearing the sprayer engage and then seeing in the rearview mirror as the fertilizer released. He focused on the path forward.

"When we get to the end of the field, I want you to turn

the plane. You can do it. Slow and steady, then return along the north side."

Skip maneuvered the plane around, feeling a rush of excitement as he did so. He grinned and held back a whoop as he headed down the other side of the field.

"Good job," said his father, nodding approvingly. "You're a natural."

6

While Liliana waited, she wandered onto the balcony and sat down on a wrought iron chair to gaze out at a lake. A white egret walked along the water's edge, on alert for prey. She thought how the fish in the water were likely unaware of the egret's long bill and deceptively quick movements. How the bird would pick them out of the water, and, despite their flapping, quickly gobble them up.

Liliana shivered despite the warm day, then glanced back to see Carlos had emerged from a back room. He held what looked like documents in his hands and waved her to come inside.

The moment she stepped indoors, a loud rapping sounded on the front door.

Carlos swung around. "Dammit! Were you followed?"

Fear constricted Liliana's throat as the knocking continued. "No. I was careful."

Carlos ran to a side table and got out a gun. He looked at her and held a finger to his lips, then walked quietly to the door. After glancing quickly through the peephole, he flattened himself against the wall and waited, gun at the ready. The rapping stopped and the visitor began rattling the doorknob. Then Liliana heard a woman's voice shout, "Hey, what are you doing?" Footsteps hurried away from the door.

Carlos glared at Liliana. "He was trying to break in. You're lucky my neighbor scared him away."

"How do you know he came for me?" asked Liliana.

"He had a cartel tattoo I would recognize anywhere. Los Tigres ring a bell?"

Liliana looked away. "I'm sorry."

Carlos got out his phone.

"Who are you calling?"

"Skip."

"No, I'm fine. We're fine. I'll just pay you and get out of your hair."

Carlos didn't answer. Instead, he rattled into the phone. "You need to come pick up your problem. Now."

"There was no reason to call Skip," said Liliana once he'd hung up. "Just give me my passport and ID."

"Skip will be here in a half hour."

Liliana withdrew some bills from her purse. "He doesn't need to be involved." She handed him the cash, with a bonus. "Just give me the documents, and I'll be on my way."

"We're going to wait for Skip. I need to know your troubles won't come knocking on my door again."

Liliana banged a fist on the table. "And how is Skip going to guarantee that?"

"He's going to see to it that I never see you again."

When they arrived at the hospital, Skip's father was awake. He was only allowed one visitor at a time, so Helen told him to go in first.

"Pop." Skip pushed a nearby chair next to the bed and sat down. "How are you feeling?"

His father filled his cheeks with air, then let out a breath.

"Why didn't you tell me sooner you haven't been feeling well?" asked Skip.

"I guess I thought I'd feel better."

Skip looked at his father's pale face. He wanted to ask about the woman who visited but decided that more stress was not what he needed. "The nurses treating you okay?" Skip reached over to give his father's hand a squeeze.

"Everyone has been great. I'm sorry to take you away from your work. I wish Helen hadn't bothered you."

"Nonsense," said Skip. "I'm here for as long as it takes for the doctors to figure this thing out."

His father began drifting off to sleep then, and Skip's phone buzzed. He got up and went into the hallway to check the screen. Carlos. Before he could say anything, his friend ordered him to retrieve Liliana. Skip agreed, then hung up the phone. He knew he should never have trusted that woman.

"How's he doing?" asked Helen, who walked up and handed him a cup of coffee.

Skip took it. "Thanks. We talked for a little bit, and then he dozed off. How much longer are visiting hours?"

Helen consulted her watch. "Another two hours."

"I need to go take care of something," said Skip. "Could I borrow your car? I'll be back before it's time to leave."

Helen looked surprised. "Okay, I'll go sit with him." She took her keys out of her purse and handed them to him.

"Thanks," said Skip. "I'm sorry to rush out."

"You do what you need to do," she said.

Skip took several big gulps of the coffee, then put the cup in a nearby trashcan and headed out.

Liliana felt a mixture of frustration at having to wait for Skip before she could get her documents and excitement at seeing him once again.

Before long there was a knock on the door and Skip called out, "It's me."

Carlos pulled open the door and checked the hallway, then waved him inside.

The two men embraced briefly, and Liliana, her nerves taut, relaxed a bit when she saw them both grin at one another.

"It's been a long time," said Carlos.

"Too long," said Skip. "Sorry about the inconvenience."

The two men turned toward Liliana, both of their brows furrowed, Skip's jaw tight.

"Can you please tell him to just give me my documents?" she implored.

Skip turned to Carlos. "She's good for the money."

"She already paid," he said, handing the documents to Skip. "I want you to walk her out of here and guarantee she won't come back. I'm transitioning out of this line of work. I did this as a favor to you."

Skip sighed. "I'm sorry. You've got my word that she or anyone else won't be returning." He turned to Liliana. "Let's go."

Liliana felt a surge of annoyance about being ordered

around and opened her mouth to protest, but then shut it and marched toward the door.

"Be careful," Carlos said as they left.

Once on the landing, she turned to Skip and held out her hand for the documents. His eyes widened and he grabbed her arm. "Follow me!" he said, yanking her forward. "The guy has a gun."

7

Skip started to lead Liliana down the back stairwell but spotted a man heading up. He turned down a dark hallway and pulled open a door that said utility room. After pulling Liliana inside with him, he locked the door.

As they stood in the tight space, Liliana pressed up against him, Skip felt her breath coming out in short, quiet gasps against his back.

"Do you think they left?" Liliana whispered.

"I think we should wait."

Liliana shifted against him, and he could smell the faint, warm scent of roses as she said softly, "Thank you."

Skip felt a mix of emotions—from irritation to relief that she was okay, to something he didn't want to admit to himself—attraction. "When we get out of here," he said. "You're going to tell me what the hell is really going on."

"I guess I owe you that much."

After some time passed, Skip unlocked the door and checked both ways, then listened. Nothing. "I think we're okay. I'm parked in the rear." He pushed open the door and they quickly made their way down the back stairs.

When they were in Helen's car and heading away from Carlos's, Liliana spoke. "I wasn't lying when I told you my father is after me."

Skip had stopped at a light and glanced over at her. "You're telling me your father is out to kill you?"

Liliana shifted in her seat. "Not exactly."

Skip rolled his eyes, then began driving through the green light.

"Those men are from the Los Tigres Cartel. You were right about that. But this all started because I was approached to be an informant for a government agency a year ago."

Skip gave a sideways glance at Liliana. "What agency?"

"The FBI."

"You expect me to believe you are an FBI agent? Aren't you supposed to be sworn to secrecy?"

Liliana looked out the window. "Not an agent, an informant. There's a difference. I don't officially work for the agency. They just want me to get information for them."

"Okay, say you really are an informant for the FBI," said Skip as he turned into the hospital parking lot. "Why not call your handler and get some protection from the cartel?"

"It's not that simple."

Skip parked in a visitor space and shut off the car, then turned to her. "What have you become so mired in you're forced to run?"

Liliana looked into his eyes, then out the window. "It's not so much what I have done as what I haven't done. What I was supposed to do."

A woman in a nursing uniform walked past the car then. "We're at the hospital. Is your father here?"

Skip ran his hands through his hair. "Yes, I need to get back in there."

Liliana reached to open the car door. "I'll get out of your way. Thanks for the save. Again."

"Where are you going to go?" asked Skip. "You're obviously not safe."

Liliana's hand tightened on the car door. "I don't know. I need to find a place to regroup. Figure out some kind of plan."

"Come into the hospital with me, and I'll help you find a hotel or something afterward."

Liliana hesitated then sighed. "Okay, thank you. I'll wait here while you visit your father."

Skip strummed his fingers on the dashboard. "I need you to go in with me. I'll just worry if you're out here."

Liliana looked somewhat relieved at Skip's suggestion. She picked up her backpack and got out of the car, then they made their way into the hospital, stopping in the lobby.

"I need to go to the ICU," said Skip.

"I'll wait in the cafeteria for you," Liliana said in a low voice, then disappeared down the hallway.

In the cafeteria, Liliana was greeted with the scent of hamburgers and French fries. It made her stomach rumble. She got in line and picked up a tray.

After washing her meal down with a soda, Liliana sat back and stared at the clock on the wall.

"Is this seat taken?" A young man pointed to the chair across from her.

Liliana glanced around to see that the place had filled up since she had sat down. Was he really looking for a place to sit, or was he there for her? She was so tired of living in paranoia. Deciding to take him at face value, she nodded her head slightly. "Go ahead."

He pulled out a chair and sat down with a tray that held a Reuben sandwich and fries. Liliana braced herself to make a run for it if he made a move, but when he began eating and made no eye contact, she calmed down.

When he finished his meal and wiped his mouth, he smiled at her. "Not bad for hospital food. Are you visiting someone here?"

"My mother," Liliana lied. "You?"

"My sister," he said, taking a sip of cola and giving her a shy smile.

Liliana chided herself for being suspicious of the young man and relaxed. They chatted for a short while as they finished their drinks.

After he left, she saw the edge of a piece of paper underneath his tray. Her heart doing flip-flops, she pulled it out as surreptitiously as possible and unfolded it in her lap. It read: *Come back to the fold.*

8

When Skip got to his father's hospital room, he was happy to see him sitting up in bed and looking more alert.

"Where'd you run off to?" his father asked him.

"Just had to take care of something. You look like you're feeling better." He sat down in the chair next to the bed.

"He's doing much better," said Helen. "They're moving him to the step-down unit tonight."

"That's great," said Skip.

His father eyed him. "You're sweating."

"It's hot out there, Pop."

"What's going on?"

"I told you. I had to take care of something."

"What do you have to take care of? You don't live here."

His father must be feeling better, thought Skip. "Fine. I could never hide anything from you. If you must know, I brought someone with me."

"Someone?" said his father, who grinned at Helen. "You didn't tell me he brought a girlfriend with him."

Helen seemed surprised. "This is news to me."

"She's not my girlfriend," said Skip quickly. "Just someone

who flew here with me." He looked from his father's to Helen's expectant faces. "Can you suggest any nearby hotels? She needs somewhere to stay tonight."

"Nonsense," said Helen. "She can stay at our house."

"No, that won't be necessary," said Skip.

"I won't hear anything else, and I'm sure your father agrees. Any friend of yours is welcome at our place. Right Mike?"

"Absolutely," agreed his father. "Where is she now?"

Skip leaned back in the chair. "Waiting in the cafeteria."

"Visiting hours are just about over," said Helen. "Why don't you get her and meet me in the parking lot?"

Skip knew when he was outnumbered. And what was he going to do, anyway? Leave Liliana in the cafeteria? "Okay fine. I'll do that."

Helen smiled. "Wonderful. We'll stop and get some take-out, and we can all have a nice dinner together. What's her name?"

Skip couldn't believe this was happening. "Liliana."

"That's a lovely name," said Helen. "I look forward to meeting her."

Skip put his hand on his father's shoulder. "Glad to see you're feeling better, Pop."

"I'm sure they're going to find it's just a bug."

On his way to the cafeteria, Skip ran through the possibilities. Most likely, Liliana would turn down the offer to stay at their house, and she'd be on her way. Who knows, maybe she already left the hospital.

But when he stepped into the cafeteria, she came out of the shadows and grabbed his arm. "I thought you'd abandoned me," she said. Her eyes were wide, and he could feel her trembling slightly.

"What happened?"

"Nothing. I just thought you left."

"Me leave a damsel in distress, not a chance," said Skip, realizing that though he sounded like he was joking, he meant it. "C'mon, we're leaving."

"Where are we going?" she said, her feet planted where she stood.

Skip said in a low voice, "My stepmother invited you to her and my father's house. So that solves your problem regarding where you're going to stay tonight. Let's go. I don't want to keep her waiting."

Liliana searched Skip's face for signs they might have gotten to him, but all she saw was sincerity mixed with annoyance.

"Are you sure?" she asked.

"To be honest, not at all. I have no idea what kind of danger you're really in, but I'm completely beat from not sleeping for two days, and my stepmother is very insistent." He turned and left the cafeteria, and Liliana followed.

When they got to the parking lot, a slight woman wearing a yellow blouse and white skirt stood by a car and waved as they approached. "You must be Liliana. It's so lovely to meet you," she said, a broad smile covering her face. "I'm Helen."

"It's very nice to meet you, Helen," said Liliana. "I appreciate the invitation."

They headed out of the parking lot, Liliana in the back seat.

"There's a wonderful Italian restaurant near the house that does takeout," said Helen, glancing over her shoulder. "Does that sound good, Liliana?"

"It sounds wonderful." Liliana wasn't about to appear rude and tell them she had already eaten.

As they drove, she sat back against the leather seat and willed her shoulders to relax. She watched and listened as Skip talked with his stepmother, noting the easy banter between them. She thought about her own family dynamics and how they were worlds different. What would it be like, she wondered, for things to be this simple and straightforward?

As Skip talked with Helen, he was keenly aware of Liliana in the back seat. He felt a mix of relief to know she was okay and irritation at himself for letting this get so out of hand. He hoped he wouldn't regret bringing Liliana into his father's and Helen's home.

When they sat down around the dining room table with the takeout, Skip found that he was hungrier than he'd first thought. He devoured his lasagna, salad, and several breadsticks and wished he'd ordered more.

As if reading his mind, Liliana pointed to her food and said, "Did you want some of mine? You seem to be hungrier than me."

When Skip gave her a dubious look, she slid her plate toward him. "The Pesto Alfredo is delicious. Try it."

Helen set down her fork and sat back and smiled, looking from Skip to Liliana. "I'm dying to know. How did you two meet?"

At the looks on their faces, she burst out laughing. "This

must be a great story. Was it on one of those online dating apps?" She put her arms on the table and leaned forward.

Skip looked at Liliana, who cleared her throat and answered. "We actually met when I, uh, chartered a flight with him."

Helen's grin got bigger. "Well, talk about kismet. You were obviously supposed to meet one another."

Skip watched, amused, as Liliana squirmed at the comment. To prevent himself from laughing, he stuffed a breadstick in his mouth.

"I guess you could say that," Liliana replied.

"Where are you from, dear?" Helen asked.

"The Pacific Northwest. Washington state, actually."

"I've always wanted to visit my namesake mountain in that area of the country," said Helen.

Skip saw Liliana give Helen the first genuine smile since he'd met her. "I hope you have the opportunity. It's a beautiful area, even if the volcano is a bit unsettling."

"It's been many years since it has erupted, hasn't it?"

"Since 1980, yes. Before that it was 1857," said Liliana.

Helen yawned. "Well, I hate to be rude, but I'm beat after the excitement of the last couple of days with your father." She got up and reached for Liliana's plate.

"Please, let me do the dishes," said Liliana, grasping her plate. "It's the least I can do."

"No arguments from me. Skip can show you where everything is. I'm going to turn in."

"Liliana can use the spare room. I'll sleep on the couch," said Skip.

"Oh, of course. Let me get you some bedding." Helen headed toward the back of the house.

When she'd left the room, Liliana said, "I can sleep on the couch."

"You take the room. I want to be near the front door."

Liliana gave him a knowing look and began gathering the dishes.

Before long, Helen returned with a pile of sheets, blankets, and a pillow, which she handed to Skip. "Sleep well," she announced.

As Liliana did the dishes, Skip made up the couch. When they both finished, he led her to the spare room. Once inside, Skip shut the door and turned to her.

"You staying here wasn't my idea," he said, suddenly aware of her closeness.

"I know," she said. "I'll leave in the morning."

"I've pulled you out of enough jams now. You at least owe me an explanation of what's really going on."

Liliana sighed. "I'll tell you. Just let me get washed up."

Skip left the room and closed the door, standing in the hallway for a moment. He heard Liliana unzip her backpack and before long the shower went on. He went back to the living room and sat down on the couch, picking up the television remote. Then he set it back down on the coffee table. He lay back as he waited. Before long, his eyes became heavy.

After Liliana had washed up, she put on her nightgown and went to the living room to find Skip asleep. As she watched his broad chest steadily rise and fall, his handsome face so peaceful, she felt disappointed. It had been a long time since she felt safe enough to confide in someone. She tiptoed over and gently pulled the blanket over him and left the room.

9

Loud knocking on the door woke Skip, who bolted up on the couch, his eyes struggling to focus in the dark. Disoriented at first, it took him a moment to remember where he was.

Helen came out into the living room then, wrapping a robe around herself. "It's five in the morning. I can't imagine who that could be." She headed for the door.

Skip sprang up from the couch. "Don't open the door."

Helen swung around; her brow furrowed.

"You just said you don't know who it could be," he said in a low voice as the thudding started again. "Let me check it out."

His stepmother nodded, her eyes wide as Skip went to the door and peered through the peephole. A woman with close-cropped dark hair stood on the other side of the door. Skip motioned for his stepmother to come over and pointed to the eyehole.

She looked through it and shook her head. "I don't know who she is," she whispered. "Maybe she's lost."

"We're not going to answer it," said Skip. He looked again to see the woman frown at the door, then walk away.

"She's gone," he said. "Maybe she was at the wrong house. Go back to bed. I'll be here."

His stepmother gave him a quizzical look and then went to her room. He was just about to go to the kitchen for a drink of water when Liliana appeared fully clothed, her backpack slung over her shoulder.

"There was a woman knocking on the door. Helen didn't recognize her."

"Did she have short, dark hair?"

"Yes, who is she?"

Liliana looked defeated. "She...it doesn't matter. There's no point." Tears of frustration welled in her eyes.

Skip reached out and took the backpack from her and pointed to the couch. "Tell me what is going on."

Liliana sat down, and he settled beside her.

"Did you sleep at all?" he asked.

"Not much."

Skip waited, listening to the rhythm of a clock. They sat that way for some time, Liliana periodically starting to speak but then stopping herself. Finally, she said, "I grew up in Washington state as I mentioned last night. My early years were wonderful, but then my mother and father got involved with this group of people." She stopped and pushed her hair back. "I didn't like the group right from the start, but my parents became enamored with the idea of living in this commune off the grid."

The revelation surprised Skip. "That must have been hard. How old were you?"

"Eight when we sold everything, including our home. I had to leave all my friends and school." Liliana took a deep breath. "I'm sorry. I find it hard to talk about this."

Moved at the struggle in her voice, Skip put his arm around her. "That's a big loss for a child," he said. "What was it like living in the commune?"

"Awful. I absolutely hated it. It turned out that my mother did, too."

"But not your father?"

"He really took to life in the commune. When I was nine, my mother left one day."

"Without you?"

Liliana's lower lip trembled. "She was there one day and gone the next. My father said that she agreed to leave me, but I've always had a hard time believing that."

"Do you know what happened to her?"

"I was told she is living on the outside, but I don't know where."

"You said your father is after you. Is he trying to get you to come back to the commune?"

Liliana nodded.

"But you're an adult. Surely he can't force you to return."

"You don't just leave. The leadership must approve a person leaving, and they rarely ever do. And there are repercussions for leaving without permission."

"What does the FBI have to do with this?"

She sighed. "They approached me a year ago via someone they had planted in the compound. Their agent could tell how dissatisfied I was with living there. I was told they would help me get out if I did what they asked."

"What did they ask?"

"They want proof the leader of the commune, Geoffrey Smelton, is being compensated for storing weapons for a nearby militant group the FBI believes is building a large-scale arsenal."

"Where does your father fit in?"

Liliana leaned her head back on the couch and closed her eyes. "He is a part of the commune's leadership. I'm praying that he isn't involved, but he could be."

So, if you do what the FBI wants, there's a possibility your father could be arrested for gun smuggling?" said Skip.

Liliana sat up. "Or worse, terrorism. The militant group is considered a direct threat to the nation."

Skip digested what Liliana had said, letting the reality of it seep in. "But how is running away going to solve anything?"

Liliana put her head in her hands. "It's not, but I don't know what else to do."

"And how does the cartel fit in?"

"When I escaped from the Holy Commune, as the cult is called, six months ago, I figured the best place to get lost was Mexico. That's how I ended up in Acapulco. I was working at a cantina as a waitress. One night after we closed, I went out back to throw away the garbage. While I was out there, I heard voices. I figured it was the owner's son coming to help him close up. But when I went back inside, I found the owner dead in the back office, the safe wide open. Then I heard what sounded like someone ransacking the cash register. I hadn't been paid for two weeks, so I grabbed a bundle of money from the safe, and on impulse, the owner's gun, which was laying on the floor next to him. I was just leaving out the back when the person saw me. He shot at me, but missed, and I started running."

"How did you know the person was a member of Los Tigres?"

"I recognized the man. He'd been in before, and one of the busboys told me he was an enforcer for the cartel."

The room was beginning to brighten as the early morning sun began streaming in from between the blinds. Liliana met Skip's eyes, her expression tormented. "So now you know why I forced you to fly me out of there. And why I'm trying to disappear."

Just then, Helen walked into the living room dressed for

the day. "You two are up early." Then she saw Liliana's backpack. "Are you leaving?"

Liliana stood. "Thank you so much for your hospitality, Helen, but I'm going to be on my way."

Helen looked to Skip, then to Liliana. "I'm not sure what is going on here, but you're welcome to stay as long as you wish, dear."

There was knocking on the door then.

Liliana picked up her backpack. "That's probably for me." She reached out her hand to Helen. "Thank you again."

Helen disregarded Liliana's hand and embraced her. "It was my pleasure. You are welcome whenever you want."

Liliana turned to Skip and gave him a small smile. "Thanks for everything."

Then she walked to the door and opened it. On the doorstep stood the woman from earlier. "I'm coming," Liliana told her, shutting the door behind her.

Helen turned to Skip, questions in her eyes. "What in the world is going on? Who was that woman?"

10

"A friend of Liliana's, I guess," said Skip.

"You guess? You don't know?"

"Like I told you, we just met."

Helen let out an exasperated breath. "You may have just met, but there is a strong connection between the two of you. Anyone can see it."

When Skip opened his mouth to reply, she held up her hand. "It's your life, and I respect your privacy. You don't need to explain yourself. I'm just sharing my observations. I'm sure you know what you're doing. Now an update on your father. I spoke to the doctor a little while ago, and he said he is doing much better and is releasing him today."

"That's great," said Skip, relieved to get the good news. "But did they figure out what the problem is?"

"The doctor said he will talk to us when we get there."

Skip grabbed his things from beside the couch. "I'll be ready in five minutes."

Once in the spare room, he smelled the faint scent of rose. Helen was right. He and Liliana did have a connection.

But now she was gone, and from what Skip could tell, walking into danger.

When they arrived at the hospital, the doctor said, "Before you go in, I'd like to speak to you both."

"Should we be sitting down for this?" asked Skip.

"The news is good, for the most part. I've already spoken to your father."

Skip let out a breath and waited.

"We've done extensive testing, and the only reason we can see for him having the problems he's been having with vertigo is low blood pressure."

"Do you know what is causing the low blood pressure?" asked Helen.

"As I mentioned, we've done a lot of tests. Heart valve problems can cause low blood pressure, but fortunately, his valves and heart are fine. It's actually a good thing you brought him in, because we're catching this early, and hopefully things can be reversed." The doctor stopped and listened for a moment as his name was called over the loudspeaker. "He appears to be pre-diabetic. Often that will cause high blood pressure, but it can also cause it to be low. With the right diet changes, he should be fine. I must go. Our hospital nutritionist will be in before he leaves to explain this all to him."

"Thank you," said Skip and Helen in unison as the doctor turned on his heels and began walking at a fast clip down the hall.

Helen let out a long breath. "Oh, my, what a relief. Your father does like his sugary desserts, but that's something we can work around."

Skip laughed. "I don't want to be around when you tell him he can't have his Eskimo Pie after dinner, but you're right, this is a big relief. We better get in there and make sure he doesn't start negotiating with the nutritionist."

When they walked in, Skip was relieved to see his father sitting up in bed, his face rosy, and his smile bright. "I guess you've heard the news. No more sweets for me."

"We did, Pop."

His father started to get out of bed. "I'm just going to get dressed, and we can get out of here."

"Stay in bed, Pop. We need to wait for the nutritionist before they'll let you out. And I'm pretty sure hospital policy is you need to leave in a wheelchair."

His father was about to protest when there was a tap on the door and it swung open. In walked a young man who looked to be in his early twenties. "Mr. Moore, I'm Arthur Tangwell, the nutritionist," he said. "After we review a few dietary matters, you get to go home."

His father eyed Arthur and the packet of papers he held in his hand. "How old are you, son?"

"Pop," Skip began.

Arthur grinned. "It's okay, I get that all the time. I'm thirty, but many people think I'm younger. I like to think it's because of good nutrition." He turned to Skip's father. "I've got some materials for you to read to better under-stand your condition, and I'm available to answer any questions."

"I think you're going to tell me no more dessert?"

"Not necessarily. There are substitutions, which these materials will explain. In addition to diet, regular exercise is very important."

His father got that obstinate look Skip knew too well. "Young man, I'll have you know that I farmed the land for forty-five years. I got plenty of exercise."

"That's commendable, sir, but you still need to get exercise."

Agent Leonardo stopped the car at a nondescript house on a tree-lined street. "You didn't say a word the whole way here."

Liliana crossed her arms over her chest. "What did you want me to say?"

The woman removed the keys from the ignition. "I know what we want you to do is hard. But it needs to be done."

"What if I refuse?"

Agent Leonardo sighed. "You know the answer to that. I have to take you into the local police station and have you charged with obstruction of justice. After that, they'll extradite you to Washington state. I really hope it doesn't come to that."

Liliana gazed out the window for some time, watching children down the street throw a softball back and forth between them. When one of them dropped the ball or overthrew, the other would laugh. How normal the interaction seemed. She had greatly enjoyed her time in the real world. Especially the comforting familiarity of the mundane. Where the FBI wanted her to return was anything but normal. Finally, she turned away from the window. "Okay, I'll go back in. But first, I have a problem with a cartel."

"We know all about your run-in with Los Tigres. It has already been handled."

Liliana was surprised. "Just like that? How?"

"Never mind how. Just rest assured they won't be bothering you again. Let's get inside the safe house so we can review the plan."

"I remember the plan."

"There have been a few changes."

"What kind of changes?"

The agent put her hand on the car door handle.

"What kind of changes?" Liliana insisted.

Agent Leonardo turned to face Liliana. "For one, Smelton is out."

"Out? What do you mean out?"

"Word is around the compound that he retired."

"No one retires," said Liliana.

"We've gathered that. But whatever happened, he's gone."

Dread gripped Liliana's stomach. "Who is in charge now?"

"Your father."

11

"Where will you go?" asked Skip's mother days before her passing. Skip was eighteen at the time.

"Go? What do you mean?"

She turned to him, her eyes keen, her breath shallow. "You're not built for the farm. Your father may not want to see it, but I know that you wish to fly. Tell me that you will soar, my son." She put her cool hand on his cheek, and Skip felt a familiar ache somewhere in his middle. He willed himself to hold back tears and forced a smile. "No one knows me like you," he said.

"That is as it should be, but in time you will meet someone, and she will also know you well."

Skip swallowed the lump in his throat. He couldn't imagine anyone knowing him as well as his mother. But he had found that what she predicted generally came true.

When they returned to the house, Skip felt a giant wave of gratitude at his father being okay. Ignoring his protests about being coddled, Helen got him settled in his armchair. When she left the room to get him a drink of water, his father turned to Skip and said, "You'll probably want to be heading out soon." Then he glanced around the condo. "Say, what happened to your friend?"

"She had to leave," said Skip, who sat down on the nearby couch.

"Too bad, I would have liked to meet her. Hopefully you'll bring her around again."

When Skip didn't reply, his father said, "Something's eating you. What is it?"

Liliana flashed across Skip's mind. "It's nothing, Pop."

"If you say so."

"I'm just glad you're okay. I was a little worried," said Skip.

"I'm not going anywhere just yet. So, how is flying going? You still enjoying it?"

Skip thought about his father's question. "I'm still enjoying it—especially when I'm on return trips after dropping off clients. There is nothing like being up in the clouds."

"Are some of the clients temperamental?"

"Sometimes," said Skip.

"So, is this it?" asked his father.

"You mean is this what I'm going to do for the rest of my life?"

"Yes."

"I'm not sure. I know I want to fly as long as I can, but whether I want to continue making a living flying people, I don't know."

"You've been in Mexico what, fifteen years now?"

"Something like that."

"I don't know, son. I always thought you'd do..." he trailed off.

Skip became irritated. "Not this again about me taking over the farm."

His father sat up straighter. "That's not what I'm talking about. I came to grips with the fact that farming wasn't for you years ago."

"Then what are you saying?" asked Skip.

His father shook his head. "I just thought that maybe you'd do more with flying, but forget I mentioned it."

Skip stood. "I've got to check voicemails."

His father nodded and picked up the remote control.

Out on the balcony, he listened to messages, including one from a frequent client who needed a flight from Acapulco to Washington DC in three days. He gazed out at the backyard, finding himself wondering once again about Liliana. Did the FBI have her headed back to the compound? Just how much danger was she in?

After several hours of reviewing her instructions for returning to the compound, Liliana said, "Enough, I get it. You want me to get proof about their affiliation with the terrorist group in the form of a paper trail by downloading the contents of the commune's computer onto this." She held up a flash drive. "What happens when I get the information? What's your overall game plan?"

Agent Leonardo didn't answer.

Anger flashed through Liliana. "If you want me to go in

and risk everything, you need to answer that question. What is the top priority? Shutting down the cult?"

"The cult is secondary," said Agent Leonardo. "Our top priority is shutting down the terrorist group. We hope the proof you obtain will prove they are stocking ammunition and a danger to the country. Then we'll go in and arrest and charge all the members. And, yes, in the process, we'll likely be shutting down the commune."

"What happens to my father?"

"He'll be punished to the full extent of the law."

"If he's involved," said Liliana.

"We're nearly certain he is, but, yes, if he's involved." She got up and poured herself a cup of coffee. "Another agent will be relieving me soon. Tomorrow morning, he'll take you to the airport. From there, another agent will pick you up and drop you at a gas station near the commune that has a payphone."

When Liliana didn't say anything, the agent said, "Look, I know this is difficult, and dangerous. I can only say that you're doing the right thing, and that our country will be grateful. As agreed, you have full immunity. Not that you've done anything wrong, but you're covered. If that is some conciliation." She carried her coffee back to the table and sat down. "What was it like growing up in the cult?"

Liliana's spine stiffened. "If you're asking if I have fond memories, I don't. It was a terrible experience from the moment my family and I arrived. Excuse me. I'm going to get some rest."

Then she marched to her room and shut the door behind her. Flinging herself onto the bed, she lay looking up at the ceiling. Before long, her thoughts wandered to Skip and their conversation earlier that day. He was so easy to talk to and made her feel understood. How she wished she could talk to him now.

12

When he finished checking his calls, Skip went into the living room and found his father dozing in his chair. As he watched him sleep, he felt bad for having gotten irritated with him earlier. He knew he meant well. The truth was Skip was more irritated with himself than anything.

When he left the farm after his mother's death to do commercial piloting, he had a vision of running a flight school. But instead, he'd settled down in Mexico and started flying individual clients. Over time, the place began to grow on him, or he began to grow on it, and he hadn't really changed course since. Lately, even though he still enjoyed flying, things had begun to ring hollow. He wanted to feel that same excitement he felt when he first started flying.

The following morning, Skip emerged from his room to find his father already up, making pancakes in the kitchen.

"Smells great, Pop, but what about your diet changes?"

"Never fear, I'm going to put strawberries on them,

instead of syrup. Get some coffee and have a seat. I'll make you one."

Skip poured himself a cup and pulled up a stool at the island. "Where's Helen?"

"She has an early morning yoga class at the park. The gals try to beat the heat." His father removed a pancake from the pan and poured in more batter. "You heading out today?"

Skip took a napkin from the dispenser on the island. "Yeah, I best get back. I need to do some maintenance on the plane before I take her out again in a couple of days. Unless you want me to stay."

"No, you've got a life to get back to. It's been nice to see you, though. Maybe you can fly in more often?" His father's back was to him as he stood at the stove, but Skip noticed a slight edge to his voice.

"Sure, I'd love to. I can aim for every couple months if that sounds good."

After removing a pancake from the griddle and plopping it on a plate, he swung around with a grin on his face. "I'd like that." He handed Skip the plate. "There's syrup in the fridge if you want some."

Skip eyed the bowl of strawberries on the island. "I'll have berries like you."

His father piled his pancake high with the red fruit, then pushed the bowl to Skip.

They ate in silence for a while, his father stopping at one point to comment, "This isn't bad."

Skip took the last bite and washed it down with coffee. "Helen told me you had a visitor the other day."

His father frowned. "Visitor?"

"A young woman. Helen said she looked to be Native American. Who was that?"

His father ran his fork along his empty plate to get the last crumbs. "Nothing you need to concern yourself with."

"If it was about Mom and her land, then it concerns me."

His father stood and reached for Skip's plate, plunking it down on top of his. "The land, the land, the land. I've been hearing about this fictitious land for years. There isn't any land. Everyone needs to just let it go."

"Everyone. Who's everyone?"

His father turned on the sink and began rinsing the dishes.

"Pop, who is everyone?"

His father shut off the sink and turned to face him. "The Sioux Council for the Dakotas, that's who. They seem to think I have some information that could help them reclaim land. That your mother gave me something. But she never did. She didn't talk about it, either."

Skip thought about the documents he had back home in Acapulco. "What if she gave it to me?"

His father raised his eyebrows. "She gave you something?"

"During her last days, she told me to get something from her chest. It turned out to be an old map and a declaration about land. She told me just to keep it. That I'd know what to do with it when the time came."

His father's expression became serious as he sat down across from Skip. "I wonder why she never told me about it, or gave me the map?"

"Maybe because whenever she brought up the subject, you shut her down."

"I didn't know she had documentation."

"More likely she didn't tell you because you're not Sioux. She said something to me that day."

"What was that?"

Skip searched his memory. "She said, promise me you'll get the land back for our people."

"Well, I'll be damned," said his father. "I steered that

young woman wrong. And after she came all the way to Florida to talk to me."

"Do you have her contact information?"

He got up and went into the living room, then pulled open a drawer and extracted a slip of paper and handed it to Skip. It read River Nelson and had a North Dakota number.

"Who knows. Maybe those papers are the answer," said Skip. "I'll give her a call."

The plane landed at Walla Walla Regional Airport in the afternoon. As planned, Liliana was taken by car to the town near the compound and dropped off. She had been given clear instructions, including checking in with the agent they'd be sending in to make kitchen deliveries. At the pay phone, she dialed the operator.

"I'd like to make a collect call."

"Number please, and who is calling."

She gave the number, then said, "Liliana."

The phone rang three times before he answered. "Yes."

"I have a collect call from Liliana. Will you accept the charges?"

There was a pause on the other end of the line, then a reply. "Yes, I accept the charges. Liliana, I've been waiting for your call. Have you come to your senses, and are you ready to pay for your wrongdoing?"

Liliana took a deep breath. "Yes, Father."

13

When Skip got to the airport, he began preparing his flight log to Mexico, but then he stopped and took out the slip of paper his father had given him. He decided to give River a call.

When a woman answered, he said, "My name is Skip Moore. You visited my father, Mike Moore, a few weeks ago in Florida. My mother was Tallulah."

"Oh, yes, I had hoped to talk to you that day, but your father told me you live out of the country."

"I do, but I happen to be in Florida right now," he said. "Could you fill me in on what the council is working on?"

"We are attempting to secure some land in the eastern part of the state. It's a small piece but significant. We have reason to believe documentation exists that can prove it belongs to the tribe and that your mother may have known about it. Does any of this mean anything to you?"

"It might."

"Since you're in the States, could you make it out here so I could explain it all to you?"

Skip quickly calculated. He could be there the following

day. And at the back of his mind, he thought about the fact that he'd be a lot closer to Washington and Liliana.

A truck came to pick Liliana up. The driver, a man with a bushy beard and wearing the commune's standard gray overalls and white shirt, took her backpack and threw it in the bed of the truck, then motioned for her to get in. He didn't say a word as he started up the vehicle and began barreling down the highway. When the compound loomed in the distance, the dread Liliana had been feeling congealed into a lead lump in her chest that made it difficult to breathe. While they waited for the electronic gate to slide open at the entrance, she willed herself to take slow, even breaths.

She looked out the window as they drove the winding dirt road to the back of the compound. At first glance, the commune appeared to be the serene wilderness refuge the leadership promised converts—a coexistence of humanity and nature. It was a lovely piece of land nestled in the woods, towering evergreens reaching toward the sky. The truck stopped before a small bridge over a stream to wait for two residents carrying baskets of blueberries to pass.

After the truck drove over the bridge, the path narrowed and the surrounding vegetation became thicker. The dense, emerald greenery enveloped the road as dappled sunlight sprinkled the way forward. They stopped in front of a large trailer. Liliana took a deep breath and got out of the truck. Her backpack would be searched and many of the personal items removed before it was returned to her. She walked up the path, paved with gravel, and opened the front door.

Skip stopped in Tennessee for his first refueling and decided to spend the night. He would rest and finish the journey tomorrow. He found a hotel near the airport and bought some takeout to eat in the room. As he took a bite of his hamburger, Liliana sprang to mind as she had been doing ever since they parted. He grabbed his phone and did a quick search for the Holy Commune and was surprised to see several articles about it.

For the next hour, he read, becoming more informed about the cult and cults in general. While he'd known cults existed, they seemed like something foreign and almost not real, but he could see now they were dangerous and preyed on people. He thought about Liliana being indoctrinated into the cult while so young. He could understand now why she had been so desperate to get away.

Liliana walked into what was considered the blessed chambers and sat down on the chair facing her father. It was odd to see him sitting behind the massive oak desk rather than Geoffrey. He wore a gray robe and a silver cross suspended from a thick chain around his neck. His close-cropped salt and pepper hair appeared grayer than just a few months before. His penetrating brown eyes, the most arresting thing about him, studied her face for some time before he spoke.

"I was glad to get your call and to hear that you reassessed and decided it was in your best interest to come back to the fold," he said.

You mean in your best interest, she felt like retorting, but held her tongue. Instead, she answered, "I realized there was no point in running."

Her father's face remained serious as he leaned back in his chair and steepled his hands. "Why have you returned?"

Liliana sat up straighter. "What happened to Geoffrey?" she countered.

Her father straightened a letter opener that lay on the desk. "He is no longer with us. I'm in charge now. Now answer my question. Why did you return?"

"I realized you were never going to stop looking for me, so I gave up and came back."

"You never just give up, Liliana."

Liliana thought about her instructions from the FBI and how important it was for her father to believe her story. She slumped forward slightly, as if defeated. "I'm tired of running, so I decided to come back. Isn't that what you wanted?"

"It is. Although I find it quite convenient now that I am in charge."

"This was news to me." She swallowed. "You spoke of my punishment for running away. Can we get on with it?"

"What is the hurry? Can't a father speak to his daughter? Tell me, what were you up to on the outside?"

"The only thing I was up to was trying to escape the compound. To no avail, obviously."

"Our people saw you in Florida in a hospital." Her father studied her further, and she waited, her heart thumping faster when she wondered if he would mention Skip. She would hate for him to get dragged into this.

When moments passed and she said nothing, her father sighed. "Very well. Though you are my daughter, I can't play favorites. You will be assigned to solitary for now. You will talk to no one. If you open your mouth to complain about anything at all, more time will be added to your punishment. Is that understood?"

Liliana nodded.

He picked up a bell on his desk and rang it. The door opened and a man walked in.

"Take her to the cell," her father ordered.

The man, who she knew to be Rick, gave her a malevolent grin as he grabbed her by the arm and pulled her to her feet.

14

"Looks like even the leader's daughter doesn't escape punishment," Rick growled as he led her down a dank hallway. He flung open a cell door and pushed her inside, slamming and locking it. One final smirk and he turned and strode back down the hallway. Soon the door to the outside opened and shut and all became quiet.

Liliana glanced around the cell, which she had only heard about but not seen until now. A bed made of plywood placed on cinderblocks sat in one corner, a makeshift toilet in the other. The only source of light was a tiny window.

All night long, Skip tossed and turned, dreaming of Liliana. He kept waking up to check the clock, only to see that mere minutes had passed. Finally, at daybreak, he got up and took a shower and dressed and checked out of his room.

At a nearby coffee shop, he drank two black coffees and ate a plate of eggs and bacon.

Just as he finished his meal, a mother, father, and a little girl came in for breakfast. He watched as the family sat down and joked as they ordered, and his thoughts went to Liliana and how different her childhood must have been. He paid for his meal, then called a rideshare to the airport. When he got there, he gave the tower his flight itinerary. Then he made a quick call to River.

"Can I expect you later today?" she asked.

"I apologize, but something has come up. I will get back to you in the next couple of days."

At a go-ahead from the tower, Skip started the plane up and got ready to taxi. If he only stopped to refuel, he could make it to Washington state by early the next morning.

It was late afternoon when Liliana heard someone enter the building and walk down the corridor. She got up from the bed and stood.

A woman she hadn't met before came to stand in front of the cell and eyed her for a few moments without speaking. Liliana knew this tactic—silence to intimidate. Well, she could also play the game. She said nothing. Finally, the woman spoke. "My name is Dr. Lydia. Interesting to meet you, Liliana."

Liliana nodded slightly. "Are you new here? I don't recall seeing you before."

Dr. Lydia smiled. "I am. Since your father took over, he has been working to improve conditions around here, and one of those improvements is assessments when members have strayed. I'm a psychologist by training. We're going to be doing your reentry interview."

"I'd invite you in, but I'm afraid my accommodations are lacking," said Liliana dryly.

The woman laughed and took keys out of the loose-fitting, gray uniform she wore. "A sense of humor, I like that. Not to worry, I'm taking you to my office where we'll get to the reason why you left the commune." She stepped aside while Liliana left the cell. Once outside, they walked down a path to a set of trailers and went into the first one. Dr. Lydia pointed to the chair sitting across from her desk and said, "Take a seat." Then she went to a side table and turned on a kettle. "I'm going to make you some tea."

Liliana watched as she opened a glass jar and spooned out a heaping teaspoon of a substance into a teapot.

"What is that?" asked Liliana.

Dr. Lydia turned to her. "Oh, just some medicinal mushrooms to help boost your energy and enhance clear thinking."

"I don't want anything mind altering," said Liliana warily.

"It won't do anything like that. It will just help clear your head." She turned back around to pour the water that had begun to boil into the cup and then carefully brought it over to Liliana. "Here you go. Once it cools, do drink up."

Liliana looked down at the concoction, which had a musty smell.

Then Dr. Lydia sat down and folded her hands on the desk. "Now, let's talk about why you chose to leave the fold. We want the truth. You can tell me whatever was bothering you that made you feel you had to leave. We're also going to talk about what you did when you were outside."

Liliana thought for a moment, then replied, "I just got stir crazy and wondered what it was like out there. Then once I got out there, I was frightened to return."

Dr. Lydia raised her eyebrows. "Frightened to return. Why ever for? Your home is here, and you are always welcome."

"I was afraid of being put in solitary," she said.

Dr. Lydia smiled, but it didn't reach her eyes. Liliana could tell she wasn't buying her story. She gestured with her head to the tea. "Have a drink, Liliana."

Liliana brought the cup to her lips and recoiled. "I'm sorry. It's still too hot."

Leaning back in her chair, Dr. Lydia said, "Very well, we'll wait until it cools."

As Skip flew west, he thought how what he was about to do was completely crazy. But he wouldn't be able to live with himself if he didn't try to help Liliana. She had been so frightened about going back to the cult that she was willing to commandeer his plane at gunpoint. And now she was going in on an extra risky mission to help the FBI. He greatly feared for her safety.

"You have such a kind heart. Don't let life take that from

you," said his mother one day after school. Skip was in seventh grade and had just gotten in a fist fight with a boy twice his size who had been bullying one of his friends. She handed him a bag of frozen peas and went to get the arnica cream to apply to the bruise quickly forming on his cheek. Wincing as he placed the cold bag on his face, Skip was surprised at her response, given that she always taught him violence wasn't the answer.

When she returned with the cream in hand, he said, "I'm sorry I got suspended, and that I won't be able to play in the game on Saturday."

She removed the bag of peas, patting the moisture from his face with a towel and taking a closer look. Then she dabbed some cream onto his cheek and gently blended it in with her fingers.

"You took a stand against hatred and ignorance. Sometimes that must be done to show the world that not everyone will watch wrongdoing without reacting." She patted his hand. "Be proud of yourself for standing up against injustice. And promise me you will always do so."

"I will, Mom, I promise." He grinned. "I might have a black eye, but you should see the other guy. I don't think he's going to bother Josh ever again. What am I going to tell Pop?"

"I'll handle your father," she said. "Now go do your homework."

15

When Skip stopped for the first refueling, he still hadn't come up with a way to get into the commune, so he gave Carlos a call.

His friend answered on the second ring. Skip could hear loud music in the background. When it was quiet, Carlos said, "Skip, what's up?"

"I've got a strange request," he said.

His friend laughed. "Any stranger than your last request?"

"Well, it's kind of related."

"Related how? This about that *chica*, Liliana?"

"Yes."

"What happened? She lose her paperwork?"

"No, nothing like that." Skip paused.

"Like what then?"

"Just bear with me. It's a long story, but she's involved in a cult, and—"

"Shit, run for the hills."

"I need to go in and help her. I know you used to live in Washington state, and I'm hoping you know someone there who could get me into the cult. It's probably a long shot, but I thought I'd try."

"As it happens, I do know someone in Spokane who could probably help you. But are you sure about this? From what I understand, you don't want to mess around with cults."

"She's in trouble."

His friend sighed. "I know you when you set your mind to something, there's no point trying to stop you. Let me make a call and see if she's available."

Skip hung up the phone and paid for his fuel while he waited. Not long after, his phone rang.

"This is Skip."

"My name is Esmerelda. Carlos gave me your number. I understand you're trying to get into a cult to rescue someone. I might be able to help you. What's the name of the cult?"

"The Holy Commune."

"I know that one. They're based north of Spokane, where I'm located."

"I'll be flying in tomorrow. Can I meet you?" asked Skip.

Liliana wasn't going to get out of drinking the tea. As she and Dr. Lydia stared one another down, she ran through her options. She could pretend to spill it, but then she'd only make her more. Just then there was a knock on the door, and she got up to answer it.

A young girl stood on the doorstep. "Dr. Lydia, Michael is acting out again. Brother Stanford told me to come get you."

"I'm in the middle of something," she told her, then

glanced back at Liliana. As she did so, Liliana pretended to take a sip.

"What should I tell Brother Stanford?"

As Dr. Lydia debated, Liliana brought the cup to her mouth again.

"Very well, I'll come right now," she said. Then she wagged a finger at Liliana. "Drink the rest while I'm gone."

As soon as she left, Liliana went to a window and pulled it open and poured the liquid in the bushes outside. Then she dashed to the teapot and half-filled the cup with water and went to sit down. Just in time, as Dr. Lydia soon came back through the door. She looked at the half-filled cup in Liliana's hands. "Go ahead and finish that and we can resume."

Liliana obliged and drank the rest of the water, then set the cup on her desk.

Dr. Lydia eyed Liliana. "How are you feeling?"

Liliana gave her a lazy smile. "Really good now. What did you want to know?"

Dr. Lydia opened a notebook. "I want to know everything that you did when you were outside. Let's start from the beginning."

"Everything? Like how I went to the lingerie department at Macy's and tried on lacy bras?" She pretended to stifle a giggle.

Dr. Lydia smiled. "Yes, everything. What else did you do? Did you speak to anyone?"

"There was a nice saleslady there."

Liliana suppressed a smile at the look of irritation that flitted across Dr. Lydia's eyes. "What about anyone who asked you about the commune and how we work?"

Liliana shook her head. "I didn't tell anyone I came from the commune. I didn't want to answer questions."

Dr. Lydia nodded. "That's good. There was no one asking about us?"

"Like I told you, I didn't want anyone to know. I was trying to live a..." She paused and looked down at her hands, which she clasped.

Dr. Lydia sat up straighter and scrutinized Liliana. "Live a what, Liliana? I need you to be truthful with me. This is very important."

Liliana blurted, "Live a normal life. I wanted to try on pretty clothing and drink wine and get kissed by a man." When she said this, Liliana thought of Skip.

"And did you do those things?"

"All but kiss a man."

Dr. Lydia gave her a small smile. "How was your experience? Did you enjoy the pretty clothing and wine?"

"At first, but then I became homesick." She frowned and continued to look at her lap.

As Dr. Lydia took notes, Liliana snuck a peek at her. It looked like maybe her act was working.

"You didn't meet any new friends?" she asked.

"No, but I tried," said Liliana.

"How did you go about trying?"

"I tried to talk to people, but it was awkward."

"Explain to me what you mean by awkward."

"I would speak to people I met, but they were going about their lives. Like I said, it was awkward."

Dr. Lydia finished writing, then closed the notebook. "Thank you for your honesty. I'm going to report the findings to leadership. Let's get you back to solitary."

It was almost six am when Skip landed in the small private airport. Esmerelda had said to call when he arrived.

At the muffled hello on the other end of the line, he said, "Hopefully this isn't too early. This is Skip."

"You're at the airport?"

"Yes."

"I'll be there in twenty."

An electric blue Nissan Leaf pulled up a few minutes later, its engine quietly whirring. The driver's side window slid down, and an attractive woman with long, ash-blond hair pulled back in a ponytail asked, "Skip?"

"That's me."

"Get in."

He opened the passenger side door and slid inside. "Thanks for picking me up."

"No problem," she said. "I've got a vested interest in rescuing people from cults, but that's a long story."

"So how do you know Carlos?" he asked.

"We used to date."

"Oh," said Skip. "I didn't know."

Esmerelda gave a sharp laugh. "That's okay, neither did Carlos." She reached into the back seat and pulled a folder out of a bag and handed it to him. "There's the lowdown on what they call the Holy Commune. I'd be very careful with them. There are reports that people have gone in and never come back out. The place is fifty acres, and the estimate is that there are about two to three hundred residents, or brothers and sisters, as they call them."

When Skip gave her an alarmed look, she said, "I'm just telling you what I've heard. There's a lot more in the file. You need to study it before you penetrate. What are you trying to accomplish, anyway?"

"I want to help someone who went back inside to obtain some information and then get her out."

"You sure she wants out?"

"I'm positive."

Esmerelda tapped a red lacquered nail on the steering wheel. "If you want to help her obtain information, going in just for the day isn't going to be enough time. I was planning on sending you in with a contact who works for the electric company, but that won't work."

She was right, Skip thought. "What do you suggest then?"

"You need to go in as a new convert."

"Wait, what?"

Esmerelda turned to him. "Make up your mind right now. You are either all in on this, or you aren't. Which is it?"

Skip didn't hesitate. "I'm in. I'll do whatever it takes."

"Buckle up," Esmerelda said and began driving. "I'm going to take you to the person who provided the file. He's a professor at Washington State and specializes in cults. He'll know how to get you invited in."

Skip opened the file, thinking that things had become very real very fast.

16

When they arrived at a cabin located at the end of a long drive, the first light of dawn bathed the two-story structure with a soft, yellow glow. A porch wrapped around the front of the house, and a delicate wisp of smoke curled from the stone chimney.

"Nice place," said Skip. "How long have you known the professor?"

"All my life," she said as she sent a text. Seconds later, her phone buzzed. "We can go in."

They got out of the car to the sounds of nature awakening, the earthy smell of forest mulch in the air. When they climbed steps and arrived at the front door, Skip expected Esmerelda to knock, but instead she pushed the door open and walked in. In the entryway stood an umbrella stand, and a table upon which lay a small stack of mail.

"You in the sunroom?" Esmerelda called out.

"Yes, back here," said a man's voice.

They walked through a hallway lined with framed photos until they came to a living room and adjoining sunroom. The door was open, and Skip could see an older man sitting at a table, a coffee cup in hand. When they entered, he stood and embraced Esmerelda. "Essie, twice in one week. I'm thrilled."

Esmerelda pulled back and smiled. "It's always good to see you, Dad." She turned to Skip. "This is the man who needs assistance infiltrating the Holy Commune. Skip, meet my father, Dr. Henrique Tarrover."

Skip reached out to shake the man's hand. "Dr. Tarrover, thank you so much for seeing me."

"You may call me Henrique," said the man, who wore horn-rimmed glasses and a red sweater vest and corduroy pants. "Please sit. Would you like some coffee? I also have homemade scones." He gestured to a basket on the table.

"Coffee would be great, if it's not too much trouble," said Skip.

"I'll get you a cup," offered Esmerelda. "How do you like it?"

"Black is fine."

Skip glanced around the sunroom. The space extended gracefully from the cabin's main structure, blending seamlessly with the outdoors. Large floor-to-ceiling windows offered a panoramic view of the surrounding forest as the early morning sun streamed through the windows, casting sprinkles of light on the wooden floor.

"This is a great space," he commented.

Henrique reached for the scones and set one on a plate. "Thank you. I find this to be a nice, quiet refuge where I do a great deal of contemplating. Now then, tell me why you'd like to get into the Holy Commune."

Skip cleared his throat. "There is a woman named Liliana who I met recently. She had escaped the commune but I believe she has since gone back inside. She is only planning on being there for a short time until she can obtain some information, and then she'll leave again. But from what I've read about cults, I think she'll need some help getting out."

Henrique took a sip of coffee. "And that's where you come in?"

Skip nodded.

"Are you currently in contact with Liliana?"

"No."

Henrique slathered butter on the scone, then eyed Skip carefully. "Before we discuss how you could infiltrate the cult, I must ask you. Are you willing to risk your life for Liliana? Because if you are discovered, you might not make it out alive."

Henrique's words stopped Skip short for a moment. Maybe it would be better to just let the FBI handle things. But would they protect Liliana in the process? He wasn't so sure. If the cult was as dangerous as it appeared, she was vulnerable. Finally, he said, "I need to go in for her."

"Very well, let's talk about what to say and to whom in order to get invited inside and considered for conversion," said Henrique.

Night turned to morning before Liliana heard someone coming down the corridor toward her cell. She sat up, her back stiff.

His posture impeccable, a deep frown on his face, her father came to stand on the other side of the bars. "I trust time alone to consider your actions has helped?"

Liliana felt a zing of irritation but repressed it. "It has, Father."

He took out keys and unlocked the door, then swung it

open. As she exited the cell, he smiled. "Welcome home, child. Breakfast is waiting in my chambers."

Liliana followed him outside to a golf cart. They boarded, and her father drove them to the far end of the property. She knew the network of trails they traversed well, as she had walked them many times. They passed clearings that welcomed in the early morning sun—some planted with vegetable gardens meant to sustain the community. In others, there were cisterns to catch and hold rainwater and open fire-pits. For a time, they rode alongside the stream dotted with moss-covered rocks. Then suddenly, the trail began to climb, and the golf cart slowed as they did so. At the end of the trail, they stopped in front of an imposing house crafted primarily of local timber. The structure featured large oval windows with expansive glass panes that sparkled in the sun. The roof was steeply pitched, and a flag with the commune's emblem flapped gently in the morning breeze. Giant flagstones led to the front door.

"This is beautiful," she said. "You live here now?"

Her father held up his arms. "Yes. My reward for faithful service. Come, I'll show you to a bathroom where you can wash up."

Liliana followed him, trying to reconcile this impressive structure with what she'd been taught since she was eight—that humble living was God's wish. In the washroom, she freshened up, drying her hands on a soft burgundy colored hand towel, its rich plushness making her feel at odds. She walked out into the hallway to a delicious aroma, which she followed down the hall toward the soft clinking of dishes. In the dining room, she found her father at the head of the table, a place set for her at the opposite end. Without speaking, she pulled out the chair and sat down.

Her father rang a bell, and a heavyset woman she recognized as Grace from the main kitchen entered the room with a tray containing freshly baked bread and bowls of oatmeal topped with blueberries. She gave them each their breakfasts, then filled their teacups with tea.

"Will that be all for now, your holiness?" she asked her father.

He nodded. "I'll ring if we need anything."

Once Grace left the dining room, Liliana forced a smile. "The meal looks very nourishing. How wonderful that we can break bread together."

Her father beamed and picked up his tea. "To my daughter's homecoming. Now you can take your rightful place next to me."

Skip spent all day learning the ins and outs of the cult as Henrique knew it. The man was considered an expert in the field because he had done extensive interviews with those who had escaped this cult and several others in the state.

After much study, Skip had memorized what he needed to say to the men and women they called the messiahs—who recruited new members. They did some of their recruiting at a diner in town. Skip would head there first thing in the morning. Henrique had warned him the cult was wary and penetrating could take time. Skip feared that time was something Liliana didn't have on her side.

17

When Skip arrived at the diner the next morning, he took a seat facing the door and ordered himself a cup of coffee and an omelet. Once he finished, the waitress asked if he wanted anything else, so he ordered a piece of pie. It was when she went to get the pie that two young men walked in and sat down at the table next to him. They wore the signature gray overalls and white shirts he'd been told was the cult's uniform.

The waitress returned with his apple pie, then noticed the two men and rolled her eyes. "Let me know if you want anything else," she said, then turned to the men. "I see you two are back." Her tone was strained. "The boss says you can't just sit there. You need to order something."

Skip spoke up. "Can you get them both a breakfast special on me?"

She whirled around. "You sure about that?"

Skip smiled. "I'm sure. Your omelets are delicious."

She shrugged and went to get them breakfast, and Skip took the opportunity to go over and sit down with them.

"I'm Skip," he said, setting his plate down and extending his hand to shake each of theirs.

"I'm Oliver, and this is Homer," said the older of the two. "Thank you, sir, for your kindness."

Skip smiled. "Like I told the waitress, their food is really good."

She returned then and plopped the plates in front of each of them, then set two forks next to the dishes and turned on her heels.

"Eat up," said Skip. "Oh, shoot, my phone is vibrating. Excuse me for a minute." He got out his cell and pretended to answer. "Hi, Megan." He paused as if listening, then raised his voice an octave. "I told you. I'm not coming home. I'm tired of everyone telling me what to do. Tell Mom and Dad to try running someone else's life. I'm going to stay out on my own."

Skip put his phone in his pocket and feigned embarrassment. "I'm sorry. That was my sister. As you probably figured out from our conversation, my family keeps trying to run my life. I used to work for the family business but I left a couple of months ago to find work and show them I'm fine on my own."

"How's that going?" asked Oliver.

Skip frowned. "Not well. I've been looking for work for a few weeks without any luck, and now I'm running low on cash."

"What do you do?" asked Oliver.

"I'm a mechanic. I can fix anything that drives or flies."

The two men looked at one another.

Skip leaned forward. "Tell me you know someone who needs something fixed."

"We might," said Oliver. "But we'd have to check. Have you ever heard of the Holy Commune? We live there."

Skip raised his eyebrows. "Is that a church or something?"

Oliver finished swallowing a mouthful of egg. "We aren't a church, but we offer a spiritual, better way of living. In fact, many of our residents are people just like you who aren't happy with the pressures put on them by family members and society as a whole."

"Wow, that sounds like a great place to live," said Skip. "How do I sign up?" He laughed. "Like I said, I can fix just about any type of vehicle."

Oliver set down his fork, his plate clean. "That's not exactly the way we work. Only residents are allowed to work for an extended period at the commune."

Skip sat back. "Oh, that's too bad."

"But," said Oliver, "we are open to new residents."

Skip smiled. "Really? That would solve all my problems. A job and a roof over my head. How do I apply?"

"We're going to have to speak to our leader," said Oliver. "If he okays you coming onto the property for an evaluation, things could work out. First, we will need some identification from you. We can't be too careful."

"Of course, I understand and appreciate that," said Skip, who pulled out the ID Esmerelda had made for him. "Will this do?"

Oliver checked it out. "Skip Harrison. You're from Nebraska."

"Yes, sir," said Skip.

Oliver copied information from the ID into a notebook and handed it back to him. "Meet us here tomorrow morning at the same time. We'll let you know what the leader said."

Skip grinned and took Oliver's hand to vigorously shake it. "Thank you. My funds are just about gone, so this couldn't have come at a better time."

After the men left the restaurant, Skip went back to his

room and paced. He'd done his best. He just had to hope his act was convincing enough. He made some calls, including arranging with another pilot to take his client in two days. Then he went to the lobby and paid a week ahead for the motel room.

The next morning, Skip headed over to the restaurant with the clothes on his back, a small amount of cash, and the fake ID. He'd been advised to not bring his cellphone onto the compound, so he left it in the motel room. Though going in with no way to contact the outside world was risky, it was the safest way to get them to believe his story. He sat down at the same table and ordered breakfast but found his stomach was so tied up in knots he could barely eat. After a third cup of coffee and moving the food around on his plate, Oliver and another man he didn't recognize walked in and approached his table. The other man scrutinized Skip.

"This is Bernard," said Oliver. "We've got good news for you. Our leader said he would like to meet you."

Skip smiled and stood. "I'm ready when you are."

Oliver nodded approvingly. "Let's go then."

He followed the two men out to a beat-up truck.

"Get in the front," said Oliver. "I'll ride in the back."

Skip did as he was told, glancing at Bernard, who didn't say anything but started the vehicle up and backed out of the parking lot and onto the highway.

"Thanks for the ride," said Skip.

Bernard remained stony faced and grunted a response.

Before long, they stopped at a tall metal gate. From this vantage point, it looked like chain link fencing topped by spools of barbed wire bordered the entire compound. They drove through the entrance and began bumping up and down a gravel road, passing wooded areas that held an occasional outbuilding. After some time, they pulled up in front of a large trailer.

Oliver and Skip got out, and Bernard drove away.

"Our leader, who you can address as your holiness, is waiting to see you," said Oliver.

18

Skip knocked on the trailer door and was told to come in. He did as instructed, entering to find a tall, imposing man waiting to greet him. He wore a long, gray robe, and a cross hung around his neck. He smiled and held out his hand, which Skip shook.

"Very nice to meet you, your holiness."

"You have a nice firm shake," said the man, who then headed to the chair behind a massive desk. "Please take a seat, and we'll get acquainted."

"That's probably because I've worked with my hands my whole life," said Skip as he sat. He studied the man's face. Was this Liliana's father?

The man put his elbows on the arms of his chair and steepled his hands. "My messiahs tell me you and your family aren't seeing eye to eye?"

Skip heaved a sigh. "They just don't understand I want to go out on my own and explore the world. I've been working for the family business for more than a decade now, and I want something of my own."

"I understand that you are low on funds," said the cult leader.

"Yes, but like I told Oliver, I am willing to work for my keep. I can fix just about any type of machinery or vehicle. I saw that your community here seems to be self-sustaining. That's my motto. Don't be dependent on anyone but yourself."

The man gave Skip a wooden smile. "We don't believe in man as an island here. We work as a community. When everyone pitches in, we all rise up."

"I like that," said Skip.

"Tell me about your upbringing. I'm told you learned to be a mechanic by working on tractors? It so happens that we have a tractor that needs some maintenance."

"I grew up on a farm in Nebraska, so farming is in my blood," said Skip.

Your holiness nodded, his eyes boring into Skip's as he did so. Was he buying what Skip was shoveling?

"What does your family grow on the farm?" he asked him.

"Corn and grains, mainly," he replied. "Our most lucrative crop is corn, but we also grow oats."

"How much acreage?"

"The farm is forty-five acres," said Skip.

"It just so happens that our ultimate goal is to grow oats," said the cult leader. "We've been hampered in meeting that goal by the fact that we have a tractor that needs fixing."

"Well, I'm your man," said Skip enthusiastically.

Not so easily convinced, the leader said, "We will see about that, but I'm willing to give it a try. I'll let you stay on a trial basis. If you can fix the tractor and coordinate the preparation of the fields, we can discuss your status here."

"Thank you so much for taking me in, your holiness," said Skip. "You won't be disappointed. I promise I'll pull my weight, starting with the equipment."

"Oliver is waiting outside to show you around the compound," he said, dismissing Skip as he consulted some papers on his desk.

Liliana was expecting further punishment but perhaps because her father was now in charge, there didn't seem to be any more repercussions for her errant ways. She was assigned to her old jobs, including working in the "library," a glorified propaganda mill composed of books approved by the leadership. That meant volumes on activities like canning, gardening, cooking, and woodwork. They also had on display in the center of the room what they considered the most important book—*Our Holy Order*, a treatise on the philosophy, rules, and regulations of the Holy Commune.

She liked library duty, as she enjoyed working alone where she had privacy and time to herself to think. She was also assigned to meal preparation duty, which was good. It got her into the kitchen where she would be able to meet with the agent who would be coming in from the town grocer.

As she shelved the recently returned books, she ran through her options for getting into her father's computer. Somehow she had to get invited back to his house. There had been no time at breakfast that morning. She would have to finagle another invitation.

She was shelving a book on crocheting when she heard voices outside. When the door to the library opened, she gasped to see who walked in with Oliver. Shock gripped Liliana, rendering her momentarily speechless. Her heart raced, as if trying to catch up with this unexpected twist of events. She blinked several times, thinking surely she was seeing things, but then Oliver said, "Skip, this is Liliana. Skip is our new trial member."

Her heart stuttering in her chest, Liliana managed to finally say, "Welcome."

"Liliana is our librarian, although she has a lot of other talents as well. Did you want to show Skip around the library? I need to check on something for your father. I'll be right back."

Liliana nodded. "Of course."

Skip waited until Oliver had disappeared down the path outside to approach Liliana. He pulled her into his arms and held her close. Finally, he let go and said, "I'm so relieved to see you."

"Skip, what are you doing here?"

"I couldn't leave you in here by yourself."

Liliana remained stupefied. No one had ever done anything like this for her.

Skip placed his hands on her shoulders. "I'm here to help you get the information so you can get out of here." He looked at her closely. "Are you okay?"

"I don't know what to say. I never thought I'd see you again. My father let you in?"

"If your father is the man in the gray robe with the cross, yes, he let me in."

Liliana saw Oliver coming down the path and quickly stepped away from Skip, then pulled a book on candle making from the shelves. "Since you like to work with your hands, you might consider making candles," she said, handing it to him. "We use a lot of them here at night."

"I see that Liliana is already introducing you to new skills," said Oliver when he walked in. "You can take the book. She'll record it. We need to continue our tour."

"Wow, that was easy," said Skip. "When do I have to return the book?"

"When you've mastered the skill," said Oliver. "See you at dinner, Liliana."

After they left, Liliana felt lightheaded. She pulled out the chair at her desk and sat down. For the first time in her life, she didn't feel alone.

19

After the tour was complete, Oliver showed Skip to what he called his sleeping quarters, which consisted of a cot in a large tent lined up next to many other cots. Stacked on the bed were three sets of overalls and white shirts.

"Those should be your size and are labeled with your name," said Oliver. "Soiled clothing is to be put in the bin in the shower room at the end of the day. The brothers and sisters who do the washing take care of that. There is a plastic crate under the bed for necessary storage. We don't ascribe to hoarding possessions."

"What do you ascribe to here?" Skip asked.

Oliver looked taken aback by the question. "Our holiness must have explained to you we are a society of oneness. That we ascribe to the state of oneness and completeness. For that reason, we all live together and work together as one."

Skip nodded. "He did explain that but I figured I'd get your take on it. How long have you lived here?"

"Ten years. I came here broken, and now I'm whole."

This guy had certainly downed the Kool-Aid, thought Skip.

"Do you have family on the outside?"

Oliver's expression became resolute. "My family is here. Those responsible for my birth are no longer my family."

Skip wanted to ask him what could have been so horrible for him to renounce his real family, but he had a feeling that wouldn't be advised.

"Supper is in thirty minutes. Everyone will be returning to quarters soon for personal reflection before the meal. We generally encourage silence and prayer during this time." He pulled a small red book out of his pocket and handed it to Skip. "Let this be your guide."

Skip took the book titled, *Our Holy Order*. "Thanks. I'll look it over," he said.

Oliver smiled. "Very well. I'll see you at supper."

Skip sat down on his cot and opened the book and began flipping through it. It was filled with rules and regulations for "holy" living and several prayers. Soon, men began to filter in, many of them looking beat and even downtrodden. He tried to make eye contact, but most of them would avert their eyes when he did so. He wondered how many of them had renounced families to live this way, and how many of them regretted doing so.

"Your aunt will be here soon with her new baby," said Skip's mother to him one crisp autumn morning on the farm. "They've named her Blue Sky."

Skip, twelve at the time, screwed up his face.

"Why that look?"

"You know they are only going to make school difficult for her naming her that. Does she have another name, too?"

Skip always knew when his mother was greatly displeased with him. She would look away and begin working frantically on whatever it was she had been doing. This time it was scrubbing the stove. He knew without her saying anything why she was angry. She felt he was dishonoring his birthright. He immediately felt ashamed.

"I'm sorry. Blue Sky is a very pretty name." And she could always change it when she grew up, he thought but didn't say.

His mother stopped scrubbing and turned to him. They met eyes for a few moments, neither speaking. Finally, she said, "One day you will want to know more about your heritage, but I will be gone."

"That's not true, I want to kno—" Skip started but his mother put up her hand to stop him. "No more talk of this now. Check to see that the living room is prepared for their arrival."

Skip's mother had been right. When he got older, he did want to know more about his heritage, but she died after he graduated from high school and had been ill much of his junior and senior year. She hadn't pushed the knowledge on him, but now he wished she had.

At dinner, Skip hoped to be able to speak to Liliana, but the men were seated apart from the women. He was able to make eye contact with her a couple of times, but that was about it. The meal, consisting of chicken raised at the compound and fresh-grown greens, was better than he expected. They began by standing and raising their hands and reciting a prayer about being glad for the harvest. As they did so, Skip glanced around to notice that while many people seemed to be fervently praying, others didn't look too enthused.

As they ate their meal, Skip was surprised to see that it was a silent affair. Apparently, you couldn't eat and talk. That squelched his idea of grilling his table mates about the place. This was proving more challenging than he had thought.

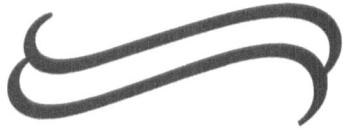

Liliana felt a sense of excitement versus trepidation about Skip being here. While she was thrilled that he came to help her, she also feared for his safety. He had no idea what went on here behind the scenes. They made eye contact a couple of times. The second time they did so, she noticed her father staring at her. After that, she kept her eyes on her plate. Her father was intuitive. She hoped he didn't sense anything more than her being interested in a new arrival.

After dinner and cleanup, Liliana was walking back to her tent when she heard voices in the shrubbery nearby. She stopped and listened. The moon was new and the sky dark, so whoever was there would likely not see her.

"Are you ready for Friday?" she heard a man say. It sounded like Oliver.

Then a woman replied, "Yes."

"Okay, good. I'll take Cantrell, as we agreed, and then you

and the others can subdue and get rid of the rest, including the daughter."

When he said the last sentence, Liliana stifled a gasp.

"We better get to our sleeping quarters before someone gets suspicious," said Oliver. Then she heard what sounded like kissing.

Before they both scurried in opposite directions, Liliana quickly stepped into the shadows. She waited for a time until the pounding of her heart in her ears subsided.

Skip had a hard time settling down for the night. He wasn't used to sleeping in a tent full of men, some of whom had started to snore. He punched up his lumpy pillow and looked up at the ceiling for a time, his thoughts turning to Liliana. She was beautiful, and at the same time remarkably resilient. He could see that now. To have grown up in this setting and not to have been broken by it, that was saying something. Skip had never been much for synchronicities or meant-to-be moments, but there was something about meeting her that made him rethink.

20

The sun streaming in from the tent flap woke Skip. He squinted and looked around to see that all the other beds had been vacated. He started to reach for his phone to check the time, then remembered he didn't have it. Sitting up on his cot, he heard a voice behind him say, "Your holiness doesn't like us to sleep past dawn."

Skip turned to see a boy of about ten, toothbrush in hand, standing there.

"Thanks for the tip," he said. "I guess I was tired."

The boy gave him a small smile. "You are new here?"

"Yes. How about you? How long have you been here?"

The boy frowned and looked down at his sandaled feet. "I don't remember. I came here with my mother and older sister."

"Are they still here?"

The boy's expression became troubled. "I haven't seen them for a while."

"What do you mean you haven't seen them for a while?" asked Skip. "Like how long?"

The boy brushed a hand across his face to hide a tear that threatened to fall. "Maybe a month." He started to say something more, but Oliver walked up.

"There you are, Skip," he said. Then he addressed the boy. "Myford, you are needed in the kitchen. Hurry up now."

The boy nodded and scurried off.

Skip stood. "Where am I needed?"

"Once you've gotten some breakfast, I'd like to show you the tractor equipment so you can get started. I'll meet you in the dining hall." Oliver started to turn to leave, but then looked Skip in the eye. "What were you and Myford discussing?"

Something told Skip not to mention what the boy had said about his mother and sister. "He was just explaining to me that it's not thought of highly to sleep once the sun has come up."

"Very good. He is correct. But we will give you a pass today."

Skip forced a smile. "Much appreciated."

Liliana hadn't slept well, the conversation between Oliver and the mystery woman replaying in her head. Now she was in the kitchen finishing up the second batch of eggs and bacon. Through the open tent flap, she spotted the delivery van from the grocer. "Look after the rest of this bacon," she said. "I'm going to get the order that just came in."

When the van door opened, she was relieved to see the FBI agent as planned.

"Morning, miss. I've come with the groceries." He walked to the back of the van and pulled the doors open.

"Good morning," said Liliana, keeping her expression even. "I expected to see Morton for the delivery."

The man pulled out a tray of bread and handed it to her. "He's feeling a bit under the weather, so he sent me. He said to tell you that he thinks you'll enjoy this new formulation of sourdough." He pulled out several jugs of milk.

"Thank you," she said. "I'm sure we will enjoy it."

The man glanced around for anyone who might be listening, then said in a low voice, "Have you made progress?"

"No, but I need to quickly. I overheard last night that a coup is planned on Friday. They plan to get rid of my father and me," she whispered.

The man's eyebrows raised. "You verified this?"

"I am sure of it."

"I will be back daily," he said. "When you have the information, I can extract you."

Just then Oliver walked up.

"Thank you so much for your attention to detail," said Liliana to the agent. "We do appreciate you counting out all of the ordered items."

"Of course, Miss. It's our policy to ensure all goes according to plan. If you could lead me to the refrigerator, I can put these milk jugs away, and we have the oatmeal you ordered."

As Liliana took him to the refrigerator, she glanced back to see Oliver observing them. Had he overheard anything?

"The engine looks to be solid, so I think it just needs a good overhaul and cleanup, and then I can have it working in no time," said Skip to Oliver. "Of course, I may need some parts. I'll know for sure once I get in and start taking things apart."

When he'd left, Skip went to the tool chest and began rifling through it hoping to find what he needed. When someone appeared behind him, he turned around to find Myford.

"I didn't hear you come up," said Skip.

"Brother Oliver has assigned me to assist you," the boy said.

"Have you worked on tractors before?"

"No, but I used to help my father with the car."

"Where is your father now?" asked Skip.

Myford frowned. "He died."

Skip felt bad for the boy. "I'm sorry to hear that. Did he die before you came here?"

Myford nodded.

Skip put a hand on his shoulder. "Well, I'm glad you're here to help me. Tractor engines aren't much different than car engines. Just a lot bigger. Want to see the engine up close?"

Skip was glad to see the boy smile.

By noon, they had the tractor engine pulled apart, and Skip had identified which parts needed refurbishment and replacing. An alarm sounded then.

"That's the lunch bell," said Myford.

Skip wiped his hands on a rag. "Go on ahead. You've earned it."

After he left, Skip was just finishing cleaning himself up

at the utility sink when he heard the door open. He swung around to see Liliana.

"Skip," she whispered, running over to him.

Overjoyed to see her, he swept her into his arms and held her close. Then, overcome with emotion, he placed his lips on hers and gave her a soft, tentative kiss. When she responded, he savored the sensation of her warm, yielding lips. It was a kiss full of promise—a declaration of the emotions they'd been dancing around since they met.

Finally, reluctantly, they broke the kiss.

Liliana's face was flushed and her smile reached her eyes, lighting up her entire face. "That was," she said softly, "wonderful."

Skip grinned. "I'm glad you think so. You have no idea how long I've been waiting to do that." Then he frowned. "I need to apologize."

"Whatever for?"

"I didn't understand how difficult living here must have been for you. I know now why you were trying to run away and disappear."

Liliana traced her finger over his furrowed brow. "There is no reason to apologize. You had no way of knowing what it's like in here. No one does, until they are here."

"There's a boy that Oliver has assigned to me. His name is Myford. He says he came here with his mother and sister, but they've been gone now for a month. What's that all about, do you know?"

Liliana frowned. "It could be that they managed to escape and haven't been able to get back in and get him. Hopefully that's the case, rather than the alternative." Her eyes became bright with unshed tears.

"The alternative?" said Skip, a lead lump forming in his gut.

Liliana sighed. "I don't know for sure if this is true, but

I've been told that when Geoffrey was in power, people were disappearing."

"Like your mother," said Skip, wishing immediately that he hadn't said anything when Liliana's face crumpled. "I'm sure she's okay," he said quickly.

Liliana took a deep breath. "I have some important news. Last night after dinner when I was returning to the women's quarters, I overheard Oliver and a woman talking. They intend to get rid of me and my father on Friday. An agent is coming back in tomorrow and can take us out of here if I get the information on the commune's computer hard drive. They believe it will show the paper trail for the arms smuggling."

"You don't need to do this," said Skip, the thought of something happening to Liliana galvanizing him. "Let's just get out of here right now. It's not worth your safety."

"I tried running, remember? It was pointless. And I can't just leave my father here to be murdered. He might have done things he shouldn't have, but he's my father."

"Okay," said Skip. "I hear you. I just wish there was some way I could help."

"Maybe there is. If I'm able to get invited to my father's house tonight for dinner, a diversion that gets him to leave for a while could help."

"I'll think of something," said Skip.

Just then there was a sound outside. Liliana ran to the only place to hide—behind the tractor.

"I thought I heard someone with you," said Oliver, looking around. "Has Myford left?"

Skip laughed. "I talk to myself sometimes. Bad habit. I sent Myford to lunch."

Oliver continued to remain vigilant, his eyes on the tractor. "How did he do?"

"He was a great help."

Oliver saw for the first time the parts lined up on an old table. "And the tractor?"

"It's in pretty good shape. To get it running, I'll need a couple of minor parts, and the rest I can clean and oil. I'll get you a list of what is needed this afternoon."

Oliver's eyes swept the barn once again, then he turned to face Skip. "Come, let's go to lunch and say a grateful prayer for this wonderful news."

Liliana stayed crouched next to the tractor for a time. When she was sure they were gone, she ran out of the barn and took a shortcut to the lunch tent. While she hurried through the backwoods, her heart hammered extra hard at the memory of her kiss with Skip.

A few minutes later as she was walking down the main path to the center of the commune, she heard a familiar voice behind her. "Liliana, do wait for us," said her father.

Stopping and turning around, she saw him walking up the path with someone. The woman wore the requisite gray dress, but unlike most of the sisters, she had a small silver cross hanging from her neck. Her jet-black hair was pulled back in a severe bun, and she gave Liliana a disapproving look.

"Hello, Father. I was hoping to have a word with you."

"Of course, what is it?"

Liliana glanced at the woman. "Alone, if we could."

"Let's not be rude, Liliana. This is Georgina, my second in command. Whatever you have to say that involves the commune, you can say in front of her."

"Nice to meet you, Georgina," she said, then turned her attention back to her father. "What I have to say doesn't directly involve the commune."

"Very well. You may go in and wait for me at the lunch table," her father said to Georgina.

The woman scowled at Liliana, then said, "As you wish."

As she flounced off, Liliana held back a gasp. It was the woman she'd heard in the woods the night before with Oliver.

21

Struggling to keep her composure, Liliana had a wild thought. Should she tell her father he was in danger?

He gave her a quizzical look. "Are you alright, child? What is it you would like to discuss?"

Liliana swallowed. "I was just wondering if we might dine together at your house tonight. Breakfast was enjoyable, but it went so quickly."

The idea seemed to please him. "What a splendid idea. I will expect you at seven sharp. Now I must go and lead the midday prayer."

That evening Liliana made her way to her father's house, running through how she might get into his study. She had the flash drive with her. Just to reassure herself it hadn't fallen out, she slipped her hand into the pocket of her dress and grasped it with her fingers.

All afternoon long, a war had raged in her mind. One moment she would decide to come clean with her father and explain that he was in danger, and the next she would decide to stick to the plan and let the FBI do what they needed to do. Finally, she decided the latter was the best course of action. She knew her father. If she told him the truth, he would refuse to believe her. He wouldn't be able to accept that the people and place he had given his loyalty to would betray him, and then he'd be in even more danger.

When she got to the door, she knocked several times. Before long, Grace opened the door. "Good evening, your father is in the dining room."

Liliana found him sitting at the end of the table. He smiled when she entered. "I hope your day was productive."

"It was, thank you." She sat down at the other end of the table. "Something smells wonderful."

"Grace is a miracle worker in the kitchen. We're going to enjoy duck tonight. Now then, tell me about your time out of the compound," he said. "What did you do?"

So that was why he'd agreed to have dinner together. He wanted to check her story.

"As I mentioned to Dr. Lydia, I went shopping and tried on clothing and ate some different foods."

"Yes, I did hear that," he said. "But wasn't there more that you aren't telling me about?"

Liliana's heart skipped a beat at his question but she kept her face expressionless. Did he know about Skip?

When she didn't say anything, he said, "My sources tell me you did some traveling."

"A bit, yes."

"Liliana, I have only always wanted what is best for you. To teach you to live a life of chaste and hard work. That's why we came here to the Holy Commune."

"I understand that Father, but I'm unclear as to your line of inquiry."

His eyes penetrated hers. "What were you doing in Mexico?" he demanded.

"I was exploring, nothing more. And when I was there, I worked as a waitress to pay my way."

"And there is nothing else you wish to tell me about your trip?"

Liliana stared her father down, finally repeating, "No, nothing else. Though the trip was exciting at first, I became weary and just wished to return home."

Her father opened his mouth to reply when Grace entered the room. "Excuse me, your holiness, there has been some commotion at the dining hall. I was told you are needed."

"Oliver is unable to take care of this?" he snapped.

"I'm relaying the message," she said. "I can hold dinner in the oven, if you'd like."

Her father threw his napkin on the table. "Very well, I will be back as soon as possible."

Once he'd left and Grace went back to the kitchen, Liliana jumped up and made her way down the hallway to her father's study.

Skip hoped he'd timed things right. He had set off the stink bomb outside the dining hall on the men's side once everyone was seated, then slipped in and sat down. Oliver was preparing to say the evening prayer before the meal when a putrid odor began wafting in from under the tent. At first, everyone remained silent, but then people started to instinctively cover their noses and mouths with napkins.

"What is that foul smell?" cried Oliver, who then ordered some of the men to investigate. "The rest of you stay seated."

Before long, a man came in from outside and whispered in Oliver's ear. They must have found the source of the stench. "I want all of the males outdoors right now," he cried. "Line up for questioning! No one is eating dinner tonight until we have a confession."

Liliana slipped into her father's office and quietly shut the door, then went to the computer. She sat down and turned it on, then saw it was password protected. After trying a couple of passwords with no luck, she stopped to think. She was likely one password away from being locked out of the system. It was then that she decided to try one more possibility. It was a long shot. She typed in March 11, her mother's birthday, and was astounded when it worked.

Sliding the flash drive into the side of the computer, she waited and watched as it began to collect all the computer's data. It was just about done when the office doorknob turned. Heart in her throat, Liliana hopped up and ran around to the front of the desk, hiding the computer with her body. The overhead light flicked on and in the doorway stood Georgina.

"What are you doing here in the dark?" she asked, her eyes narrowing.

Liliana leaned against the desk. "I was just looking for a piece of paper and a pencil."

"In the dark?" The woman began walking toward Liliana.

"I know that we are supposed to conserve energy, and I could see well enough," she said.

Georgina scowled. "I don't believe you."

"I don't care if you believe me. That's what I was doing. I can be in my father's office if I wish."

Georgina's eyes flashed anger. "I am second in command here. I have more authority than you do."

"What is this?" asked her father from the doorway.

As Georgina turned to look at him, Liliana reached back and pulled the flash drive from the computer and closed it.

"I found her snooping around in your office."

"Is that true?" he asked Liliana.

"Like I told her, I was simply looking for a piece of paper and a pencil. I had some ideas about improving the library that I wanted to jot down."

"Very well, I always encourage productivity," he said.

"But—" Georgina began.

"Why aren't you at dinner?" he asked.

"I was, but with all of the commotion, I thought I'd come check in with you."

"You can go back to dinner. Everything has been handled."

As she headed out the door, she glanced at her father's desk and back at Liliana, then stomped out of the room.

"Is the emergency at the hall dealt with?" she asked her father as they left his office and he shut off the light.

"Yes. It turns out that a new resident thought it would be amusing to create a stink bomb. He has been reprimanded."

"A new resident?"

"Yes, a man who came here to fix our tractor. I've had him put in solitary. He must learn our ways."

115

22

When it became apparent Liliana's father thought Myford was responsible for the stink bomb because the poor kid stood there shaking and unable to speak, Skip confessed. "It was me. I thought it would be funny, but apparently I misunderstood how things work around here. I'm sorry for the disruption."

Liliana's father gave him a stern look and intoned, "We do not abide by disruptions here, Brother Harrison. They take us away from our purpose. You have been given a chance here, and you have taken a misguided step." He gestured to one of the men. "Take him to solitary."

A burly guy who smelled of sweat grabbed Skip by the arm and jerked him away from the crowd down a dirt path.

As she followed her father down the hallway back to the

dining room, she slid the flash drive into her pocket. After they sat down, Gloria placed their plates in front of them.

Then he gave her an uncharacteristically gentle look. "Before I say grace, tell me, Liliana, how are you really doing? You say the trip outside didn't affect you, but you appear unsettled."

Liliana kept her eyes on her father's. "As I mentioned, though I sought experiences on the outside, they were not what I expected."

Her father appeared pleased at her response. "It took you leaving the fold to find out how much better it is in here for you, then?"

Liliana looked down at her plate, hiding the outrage she was sure showed on her face. She took a deep breath, then raised her head. "I did a lot of thinking on the outside, and I realized that family matters more than beautiful clothing. I also thought of Mother. Where is she, Father?"

His brow furrowed. "It has been some time since you asked about your mother. What prompted that?"

Liliana decided to be truthful. "When I was shopping, I saw mothers and daughters enjoying one another—laughing and talking. I couldn't help but think of my own mother. You never told me what happened. Why she left the fold."

Her father contemplated for a moment, then sat back. "I suppose you have a right to know what occurred. Your mother was a complicated woman. When we first came to the commune, she was very involved and believed in what we stood for. But over time, her views changed, and she wanted to leave."

"Where did she leave to?"

"I'm not at liberty to divulge her whereabouts, but you can be assured that she is well."

Fury scorched Liliana. "She is well without her only child, her daughter?"

Her father sighed. "In order to be able to leave the commune, the leadership at the time decided she would have to renounce all ties with you."

Liliana tried to imagine how her mother could do that, but as always, she couldn't see her willingly leaving Liliana behind.

"Who was in charge when mother left? Was it during Geoffrey's time?"

Her father nodded.

"So, you don't know for sure that where they took Mother is safe and comfortable."

Her father's frown deepened. "I was told by the leadership that she was safe and well and abiding by her end of the bargain."

Liliana could not believe her father's unrelenting blind faith in the cult. She wanted to slap him across the face and shake him by the shoulders for his foolishness. But she restrained herself.

After a few moments of silence, her father said, "All I and your mother, when she was here, have wanted for you is to be your best self. We agreed that living here in the safety of the commune away from the evils of the world was the right thing for you."

How Liliana wanted to scream at him that it was the worst possible decision for her, but she remained silent.

"Enough talk," he said. "Let us say grace and enjoy this bountiful meal."

As the night closed in, Skip lay on the hard bed in the

solitary cell, his mind whirring over what could be happening with Liliana. He prayed she had been successful in getting the information and was now safely in her bed. Just as he was dozing off, he heard his name called out. Sitting up on the cot, he said in a loud whisper, "Liliana?"

"Over here by the little window near the ceiling," she said in a low voice.

Skip got up and felt his way along the wall until a fresh breeze hit his face. He looked up to see a dark shadow above.

"How did it go?" he asked.

"It went well. I want to give you the flash drive just in case. Georgina caught me in my father's office, and I'm afraid she'll whisper in his ear, and I'll be searched."

"I was searched before they locked me in here, so that's probably a good idea to give it to me."

"I'm going to reach down with it," said Liliana.

Skip stood on tiptoe, stretching his arm upward until his fingers touched metal. "I've got it," he said as he grasped it in his hand. "What next?"

"They will likely let you out sometime tomorrow since this was your first infraction. If you can meet me in the kitchen before dinner and give it to me, I can pass it on to the agent when he comes, and then he can get us out of here."

"You can count on me," he said.

Liliana was quiet for a moment. "I don't know what to say. I really appreciate you helping me. No one ever has."

"No one at all?"

"Well, yes, someone did—my mother. Tonight, I asked my father where she is. His response was that she is safe, but I don't know if I believe that to be true."

Just then there were voices outside, and Liliana was gone.

23

The next morning as Liliana worked in the library dusting bookshelves and dealing with the occasional visitor, she kept checking the clock. She hoped she was right about them letting Skip out of solitary today.

Right before the lunch bell, she glanced out the library window to see Georgina and Oliver marching up the path toward the door. Determined to act as naturally as possible, she continued shelving books until they entered. When they did, she looked up, feigning surprise. "Welcome, Georgina and Oliver. Did you want to check out some books?"

Georgina stood in the doorway and barked, "You are wanted in front of leadership, Liliana. Come with us."

"What for?"

"Just come with us now," she said. "Oliver, please escort her."

As Liliana had predicted, they let Skip out of solitary that afternoon. He was told to go back to the barn. For the rest of the day as he worked on the tractor, he stopped periodically to gaze at the spot where he and Liliana had kissed. Every time he heard a noise, he expected her to show up at the door for the flash drive, but she never came.

Later, when Skip went to the dining hall during dinner preparations and still couldn't find her, his concern shifted to panic. She should be here by now. When one of the women in the kitchen noticed him just standing there, he grabbed a knife and began helping to cut the vegetables. He continued that way for the next hour, blending in by making himself useful.

Finally, just before dinner, a man came walking into the kitchen, his arms laden with a large bag of flour. Skip set down the potato peeler and rushed over to take it from him.

"Here, let me help you," he said, trying to make eye contact with the man, who was glancing around the kitchen. "Are you looking for someone?"

"Yes, the young woman who usually helps me with putting away the food."

"I think you mean Liliana?" said Skip, giving him a pointed look.

"Yes, that's her."

"She's not here right now, but she told me about the muffins you were going to bring. And I believe she was going to give you a recipe."

The man kept his voice even. "Yes, that's right."

Skip pulled the flash drive out of his pocket and surreptitiously passed it to him. "I believe this will give you all you need," he said.

The man nodded knowingly. "And you are?" he asked.

"My name is Skip, and I'm a new member here," he said.

The man nodded, then said as Oliver approached. "Very well, then. Thank you for offering to unload. It does my back good to get the help."

"Being of service, I see, Skip," said Oliver. "Looks like commune life is doing you good." He turned his attention to the agent. "I don't believe we've met. I'm Oliver, third in command here." He reached out his hand.

The agent took it and shook. "Very good to meet you. I best be on my way. One more delivery tonight."

Oliver watched the man leave, his eyes wary. Then he turned to Skip. "I heard you talking about Liliana."

"He was saying that she had ordered some muffins, but they didn't have any this time."

Oliver raised his eyebrows. "We don't allow sweet breads here." He pulled out his walkie talkie. Was he going to have the van stopped at the guard gate? Skip couldn't let that happen.

"Maybe I misheard him," said Skip. "It could have been that she ordered a different type of bread. Like rye, maybe, or oat or sourdough. I understand that the plans are once the tractor is working you'll be planting oats here. It turns out that I know all about growing oats."

"That's good news," said Oliver, who motioned to press the button on the walkie talkie. "If you'll excuse me."

"Wait!" cried Skip. "I have a question for you."

Oliver's jaw tightened. "Yes, Skip, what is it?"

"Did you have a chance to talk to his holiness about the tractor? The sooner we get the new parts, the sooner I can have the tractor up and running. I think it's really going to do a good job at tilling the land."

"I have not yet. He's been busy. Now, please excuse me." He turned away and pressed the walkie talkie. It crackled, and he heard a man say, "Yes."

"Has the grocery van passed through the front gate yet?"

More crackling and Skip heard the man say affirmative.

"Okay, thank you."

The flash drive was safely out of the compound, but where was Liliana?

24

Liliana was thrown in a small room in her father's house. She'd been there for hours. She looked out the window with dismay to see the sun setting. That meant the agent had already come and gone.

Finally, Georgina entered the room and motioned for her to get up and follow her. She heard voices as they made their way down the hall toward the living room. She struggled to keep her breathing even. Had they started the coup earlier than planned?

When she walked in, she was shocked to see her father bound to a chair. There was a table at which sat Oliver and another male cult member—a fat, bald man.

"What is going on?" she asked.

Georgina grabbed her by the shoulders, forcing her to sit in a chair next to her father. "Sit still, and we won't bind you."

She looked at her father, then back at Oliver and the man at the table. "I don't understand."

The fat man hit a gavel on the table. "We are in the process of reviewing the offenses as stated."

"What offenses?" She turned to her father, who wouldn't meet her eyes. "Father?"

Oliver stood and cleared his throat, then began reading from a piece of paper he held. "Brother Cantrell is hereby being charged with gross misconduct."

Liliana's breath began to come in short gasps. Was this their end?

"Offenses are hereby listed. Number one: Failure to abide by outside agreements, leading to potential bankruptcy of the commune. Number two: Making unilateral decisions without getting prior approval from leadership. Number three: Failure to appropriately punish his offspring, Sister Liliana Cantrell, for leaving the fold without prior approval, and for her current offense, engaging in a sexual act with a new convert."

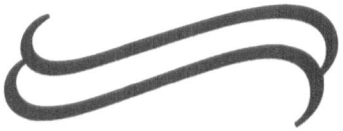

As they sat down to dinner, Skip could tell something was amiss. Liliana still hadn't shown up, and Oliver wasn't anywhere in sight. Liliana's father also failed to come say the evening prayer like he always did.

Skip pushed the food around on his plate, his worry about Liliana mounting. Finally, unable to just sit there any longer, he left the table. When someone asked where he was going, he said he didn't feel well and needed some air. That wasn't far from the truth.

Outside, he headed for Liliana's father's place. She had to be there. But just as he was rounding a corner, pain seared the back of his head and everything went dark.

After they had finished declaring Liliana and her father guilty, the fat man, Oliver, and Georgina walked to the door.

"Where are you going?" cried Liliana.

The man didn't answer. He left the room, followed by Georgina. But Oliver came to stand in front of them, a smirk on his face. "The leadership team will adjourn to the dining room to determine your sentencing," he said.

"How could you, Oliver?" cried Liliana. "My father trusted you, and this is how you repay him."

"If you were smart like your father, you would keep your mouth shut. And tsk, tsk, Liliana, seducing a new convert. He came here to help us with our tractor equipment, and now you've led him astray. He is being dealt with as well."

"What have you done with him?" cried Liliana.

"We will also be discussing who will take over the commune," Oliver said, ignoring her question about Skip.

When he left, Liliana turned to her father. "Are you going to stand for this?"

"Leadership is doing what they see as best," he said.

"What are the punishments for? What do they mean when they say you haven't abided by outside agreements and the commune is facing bankruptcy?"

"There were some questionable dealings when Geoffrey was here with dangerous people. When I took over, I refused to continue with them."

"We need to get out of here," said Liliana. "You can't be faulted for doing the right thing."

Her father didn't reply.

"Your blind loyalty is going to get you killed," said Liliana.

"Father, please, let me untie you so we can get out of here."
When he didn't respond, she asked, "Where would they have
taken Skip? To solitary?"

Her father shook his head. "No, most likely to the
stockade."

Liliana gasped. "Where they used to keep the animals?"
She stood. "I'm not sticking around for this. I need to get
Skip. He was just trying to help me."

"Please, sit, Liliana, and await punishment."

"I can't. I don't agree with any of this. If you won't go
with me, I'm going alone." She began to head toward the
door.

"They have a guard posted in the hallway," he said. "If you
must leave, go out the window. That will give you more of a
head start."

Liliana hesitated, knowing that leaving was only going to
make her father's punishment more severe. But she had to
get to Skip. She ran to the window and eased it open and slid
out, closing it quietly behind her. Then she made a dash for
the forest and began running to the back of the property,
hoping, praying, she would reach Skip in time.

25

Skip awoke to find himself lying on his side, his feet and hands bound, his head pounding. He tried to focus in the dim light. Finally, his eyes adjusted, and he saw that he was in the middle of an unused pigsty. He struggled to sit up, but dizziness caused him to lie back down. Closing his eyes, he took deep breaths in an attempt to calm the vertigo. Then he worked to get his hands free, but whoever had secured them had done a good job. When he was lying there catching his breath before trying again to get free, he heard someone approaching.

"Skip!" called out Liliana. "Are you there?"

"In the pigsty," he cried.

Soon she was by his side. "Thank god you're okay. I was so worried about you," she said as she freed his hands.

He began untying his ankles. "Where were you?"

"The leadership team, consisting of Oliver, Georgina, and some man I've never seen before, just tried and convicted me and my father. They're sentencing us now."

Skip stood and pulled her close. "How did you get away?"

"I climbed out the window. Were you able to give the agent the flash drive?"

"Yes," said Skip.

Liliana's body visibly sagged against his.

"From what you're telling me, things are unraveling fast. We better get off the grounds," said Skip.

"We're at the back of the property near the fence and a highway, but there's the barbed wire," said Liliana.

"Don't worry about that. Just lead me to the fence."

As they exited the stockade, voices sounded in the distance. Skip grabbed her hand. "Let's go."

They ran toward the back of the property under the dark, moonless sky. Before long, the shouting got closer. "Run faster," Skip urged.

When they got to the fence topped with barbed wire, Liliana cried, "We're stuck."

"No, we aren't. I've done this before. Scale the fence and then step directly on top of the wire and swing your other leg over and jump. I'll show you."

At the cries in the distance, Liliana knew the cult members were gaining on them fast. She followed Skip up as he scaled the fence, then watched when he reached the top and stepped on the wire with one foot, then stood and swung the other over and jumped to safety.

"You can do it," he encouraged her.

Heart slamming against her ribcage, Liliana placed her foot on the barbed wire and tried to stand but she was afraid to let go of the fence.

"Grab the top of the pole," Skip said.

Taking a deep breath, she let go and grabbed the pole, then pulled herself up and flung her other leg over the fence. The shouts were close when she jumped to the other side, landing on her hands and knees on the hard earth. Skip helped her up as the cult members reached the fence, then pulled her forward, shouting, "Tuck and roll," right before they began tumbling down an embankment. When they landed at the bottom in a pile of rocks, he pulled her to her feet. "Are you okay?"

"I think so," said Liliana.

"We have to keep moving."

They scrambled up the other side of the embankment, then ran several yards to the highway just as a truck approached. At first, Liliana feared it might be a member of the cult but she saw the man wore a red shirt, and she didn't recognize him. He stopped and called out of the passenger side window. "You two need help?"

"We rolled our car a ways back," said Skip. "Could you take us into town?"

"Sure, get on in."

Skip slid in next to the man and Liliana got in and slammed the door. It was then she noticed blood on her hands and tried to wipe it on her skirt.

"You're hurt," said the man, reaching into the glove compartment and pulling out a rag and handing it to her. "You folks sure I don't need to take you to the hospital?"

"I'll be okay," said Liliana. "I think the cut is superficial."

"If you can drop us off at the Outback Motel that would be great," said Skip.

"Alright, then," he said as he started down the highway. "Where you folks from?"

"North Dakota," said Skip.

"You're a ways from home."

"Yes, we are," said Skip. "It so happens, we're on our honeymoon."

The man laughed. "Well, I guess you'll have quite a story for your kids one day."

A few minutes later, he let them out at the motel, wishing them well. As he pulled away, Skip asked, "Are you sure you're okay?"

"My hand is killing me, and I'm sure I have bruises all over, but I'm okay. How'd you learn to do all that, anyway?"

"Me and my friends used to go cow tipping at neighboring farms. We had to make a lot of speedy getaways."

"Cow tipping?"

"It's a nasty sport I'm not proud of. C'mon, let's get you to the room so we can clean up that hand."

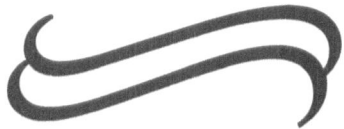

Skip got a key at the front desk, then they went into the room. He led Liliana to the bathroom and unwrapped her hand. She turned her head as he examined it.

"The good news is that you were right. The cuts aren't very deep. But the bad news is there are a lot of them. I'm going to wash them out with soap, and then we're going to need to get your hand bandaged up with some antibiotic ointment."

Liliana winced as he soaped up her wounds and washed them off. "I'm sorry for the trouble. I should be doing this myself," she said.

Skip took a hand towel off the ring on the wall and began dabbing gently at her hand. "You don't have to do everything yourself. I would think after tonight, you could see that."

Liliana was quiet for a moment. "I'm beginning to see that thanks to you." She took her free hand and caressed his forehead with her fingertips. "How's your head?"

"I've got a pretty bad headache. But I'm counting myself lucky. Things would have been much worse if you didn't show up."

"We make a pretty good team, don't we?" She gave him a small smile.

"We do. I'm so glad you're out of that place, Liliana."

Liliana got a pained expression. "But my father is still there."

Skip gently placed his hands on her shoulders. "He made his choices. There was nothing you could do."

When tears sprang to her eyes, he wiped them away with his thumbs. "Now that the FBI has the flash drive, they should be going in, right?"

Liliana drew in a ragged breath. "If the flash drive has what they need, yes."

"I'm going to run to the market down the street and get bandages and some other supplies. I'll be back shortly. Are you going to be alright?"

Liliana nodded. "I'll be fine."

Skip returned a few minutes later with a grocery bag and set it on the table where Liliana sat.

"I've got everything we need. Bandages," he said, pulling them out and placing them on the table. "Gauze, antibiotic cream, aspirin, and a few snacks and something to drink."

Skip held up the wine in one hand and the bandages in the other. "Which first?"

"Bandage."

"Practical. I like that."

He set the bottle down and opened the antibiotic cream, then dabbed some on the wounds and covered them with a large bandage that he further secured with gauze.

"You do such a good job. Like an expert," said Liliana.

"Thanks to my mother. She was a whiz at bandaging up wounds and getting them to heal. Although I don't have the herbal remedies she would make. The antibiotic cream will have to do."

"Tell me about your mother. What was she like?"

Skip smiled and sat down at the table. "My mother was the essence of regal. She was a proud woman, but at the same time she was kind and wise and very strong. I could always count on her for good advice."

"She sounds wonderful."

"What about your mother?" he asked.

Liliana sighed. "Although I loved my mother, I am sad to say she wasn't anything like yours. She was weak and easily swayed."

"I bet she loved you, though."

"Yes, I do believe she loved me."

"There had to be some good times."

Liliana thought back to her childhood. "We used to bake cookies together. Her favorite was peanut butter and mine was chocolate chip, so we'd make peanut butter chocolate chip. That was before we went to the commune, when I still had a real home."

"You deserve a home," said Skip. "Everyone does." He held up the bottle of wine. "It's a screw cap, so I can't vouch for the quality."

"I'm sure it's perfect," said Liliana, who rose and went to get two glasses, then held them both for Skip to fill.

"What shall we toast to?" she asked.

"To successfully climbing barbed wire fences without too much damage."

Liliana laughed as they clinked their glasses.

"You don't do that much," he said after he'd taken a drink of wine.

"What?"

"Laugh. It's nice when you do. I like it."

Liliana frowned. "I guess I haven't had all that much to laugh about."

Skip set down his glass and took Liliana's. "I'd like to change that if you'll let me."

26

Liliana felt her breath catch in anticipation as Skip gently brushed a stray hair from her face and tucked it behind her ear. His eyes, deep pools of warmth and need, made her heart race.

"I never thought I'd find someone like you," he said, his voice low and tender.

"What am I like?"

He leaned in closer, his breath warm against her cheek. "You're like a gorgeous star fallen from the sky—a dream I never knew I had."

Their lips met in an electric kiss that awakened her senses. As their bodies drew together, Liliana could feel the heat of their connection growing with each passing moment. When he cupped her breasts in his hands, she felt an intense shiver of desire that left her breathless. He swooped her up in his arms and carried her to the bed and gently set her down. Then he kneeled on the bed and slowly unbuttoned the front of her dress, his eyes holding hers. When he unclipped and removed her bra, she suddenly felt shy at the intensity of his gaze and looked away.

Skip responded by tenderly turning her face to his once again. "Is this what you want?" he asked her.

Liliana nodded, the desire she felt for this man deep in her soul undeniable. "I want you to be my first," she said softly.

When Liliana gave him the go-ahead, her eyes shimmering with emotion, Skip was filled with a need to please her that he had never felt with any other woman. Her giving him something so precious filled him with emotions he had never felt before. He knew that he wanted to be the one to make her smile every day.

Skip reached up and pulled off his T-shirt, then ran a finger around her breast. "You're so beautiful," he told her.

Liliana breathed, "Thank you."

Then he stood and removed his pants and underwear and kneeled over her. When she took his penis in the palms of her hands, he had a sharp intake of breath as he grew even harder. He traced his fingers around the top of her panties, then explored her velvety softness. When he did, Liliana gasped and moaned his name.

He mounted her then and entered slowly. At first, she stiffened, but then she shifted her hips and welcomed him fully. As their bodies became one in a poetic dance of desire, Skip thought his heart might burst. He held himself at bay until she cried out and came, then Skip released in a long shudder of passion. As he did so, he whispered in her ear, "Liliana, I love you." When she didn't respond, he lay down next to her and asked, "I didn't hurt you, did I?"

"No, I'm fine," she said. "It was beautiful. Much better than I ever imagined." She took his hand and set it on her chest, and he could feel her heart still beating quickly.

They lay that way for a time in silence, until Liliana said, "I'm going to take a shower."

He watched as she went into the bathroom and shut the door.

Liliana looked at herself in the bathroom mirror, the words Skip had whispered in her ear replaying in her mind. He had told her he loved her. That was something she never expected to hear. And something she had no idea how to answer.

She turned on the shower and went in to stand under the warm, running water. After a time, she picked up the hotel-sized bottle of shampoo and began lathering her hair.

When they had both finished showering, Skip reached into the bag and pulled out granola bars and chips. "Not the best dinner, but this will have to do," he said.

They sat in silence for a time, snacking. Finally, Skip broke the silence and said, "You're quiet."

Liliana took a sip of wine. "I just can't stop thinking about my father and what they'll do to him at the compound, if they haven't already. When they were announcing our infractions, one of his crimes was not agreeing to do the bidding of outsiders. He told me when we were alone that when he took over, he refused to continue doing business with dangerous outsiders."

"That's good news," said Skip. "Those facts will show in the computer files. The FBI is probably on their way to the compound right now or will be soon. We just need to wait. You'll see. It'll all work out." He crumpled the chip bag and threw it into the nearby trashcan. "It's been a really long day. Let's get some sleep. I guarantee we'll have good news by morning."

All night long, Liliana tossed and turned and dreamed about her father. Just before daybreak, she awoke, feeling a deep sense of sadness at never seeing him again. She slid out of bed while Skip slept and quietly dressed. Then she got the keys to the rental car. Before leaving the hotel room, she wrote Skip a note and placed it on the bedside table.

Stopping for a moment to watch him sleep, his face peaceful, she whispered, "I love you, too." Then she slipped out of the hotel room and got into the car and started the engine. She wasn't sure what she was going to do, but she knew she would never forgive herself if she didn't try to help her father.

Skip opened his eyes to early morning light ricocheting

from underneath the motel curtains. The place next to him was empty. "Liliana?" he called out. He sat up in bed and spied the note on the bedside table. His heart jumping into his throat, he grabbed it and read: *I have to go and see if I can get my father to leave the commune. Please stay here. I wouldn't forgive myself if something happened to you.*"

"Dammit, Liliana," cried Skip, slapping the note back onto the table. Just then his phone buzzed. He grabbed it. *Unknown number.* "Hello?"

"Is this Skip Moore?" said a woman's voice.

"Yes, who is this?"

"This is Agent Leonardo from the FBI. We're trying to get a hold of Liliana. Do you know where she is?"

"She's walking straight into the fire, that's where she is. We escaped from the compound last night, and she's going back in now to try and save her father."

"That's not good. When did she leave?"

Skip checked the clock, which read six am. "I'm not sure. I was asleep, but probably within the last couple of hours."

"We have reason to believe her life is in danger."

"I know it's in danger. We barely got out of there alive last night. A man named Oliver wants her and her father dead."

"Oliver is Liliana's half-brother," said the agent. "And yes, our intel shows that he will get rid of her the first chance he gets."

"Her half-brother?"

"Yes, that just came to light."

"You have the flash drive of the computer files I gave your agent. I thought you were going into the compound?"

"We are planning on it but are awaiting a judge to approve the warrant. He gets in at seven, at which point we'll breach."

"But that's an hour from now!"

"Hold tight, Mr. Moore. We'll keep you posted."

Skip hung up and began getting dressed. He wasn't about to stay put. He had to warn Liliana about her brother.

27

Skip called for a rideshare and had the driver drop him off near the fence at the back of the compound and entered the property. As he started running through the field they had crossed just hours before, he heard screams in the distance. It looked like all hell had broken loose, and by now Liliana was right in the middle of it.

When Liliana arrived at the compound, she was surprised to find the front gate wide open and no one manning it. She drove the car in, stopping when she reached the dining hall. Jumping out, she rushed inside the tent, expecting to see brothers and sisters preparing the morning meal, but it was empty. It was then that she smelled fire.

She ran outside and checked the horizon, seeing billows of smoke in the area of her father's house. Spotting a golf cart, she hopped on it and sped down the path leading to his place. The closer she got, the thicker the smoke became. By the time she reached his house, she found herself coughing. Looking up, she saw smoke coming from the second story. She ran to the front door but found it locked, so she hurried to the back and pushed up the window and went inside. The chair where her father had been sitting the night before lay on its side, but he was nowhere to be seen.

Covering her mouth with the top of her dress, she ran around flinging closet doors open, then made her way down the hall. No one in the dining room, either. In the entryway, she stopped to look upstairs and heard a crackling noise from above.

"Father!" she cried, putting her hand on the banister.

"No point in going up there," a familiar voice said from behind. "Your father has been taken care of."

Liliana swung around to see Oliver standing there.

"What have you done!" she cried, backing up at the strange look on his face and hitting her heel on the stairs. "Tell me he has been brought to safety."

Oliver sneered at her. "You are so obtuse, big sister. But then you always have been."

"Big sister? What do you mean?" Liliana was stunned.

Oliver approached, his eyes menacing and his fists clenched. "I meant just what I said. I'm your younger brother, Liliana. The bastard our mother gave birth to and abandoned." He gestured around the room. "All of this should have been mine, but your father was planning on giving it to you, even after you betrayed the commune. I've given the last ten years to this place, and that was his thanks. So, I'm destroying it all."

"You set the fire?" Liliana asked, horrified. "Where is my father? Please tell me, Oliver."

He grabbed her by the arm in a vice grip and yanked her

toward the kitchen. "I'll show you exactly where your father is. We're going to him right now. He's in the basement. Very soon, the upstairs will collapse, and you'll both be buried together for all eternity."

Skip made his way through the compound, trying his best to stay in the shadows. There were people running about, looks of terror and confusion on their faces. Many were fleeing toward the entrance. He headed toward Liliana's father's house. When he was near, he heard a familiar voice—Oliver. He crept up as close as he could and strained to listen.

"I was beginning to worry," said a woman. "Did you take care of the old man?"

Oliver snickered. "Even better, I also took care of Liliana. The idiot came back to save dear old dad. Now they'll both be engulfed in flames in no time. I have gasoline strategically placed throughout the house."

"Let's get out of here," said the woman. "I want to be long gone when the place blows."

After they headed down the path in the opposite direction, Skip raced toward the house. When he came to the clearing, he looked up at the second story and his heart seized. The entire floor was ablaze. Spotting a garden hose, he turned it on and sprayed himself, then ran to the front door, which was ajar. He kicked it open and went in.

"Father, are you okay?" Liliana found him slumped over in a corner of the basement. "Get up, we need to get out of here."

"There is no way out," he mumbled. He had been beaten badly. One eye was swollen shut, and his arm was bleeding.

Liliana glanced around the basement in the dim light. "Do you have any tools down here?"

Her father thought for a moment and then exclaimed, "Yes, there is an axe with the holiday things in the corner. To cut down trees."

Liliana rushed over and began throwing boxes of ornaments aside until she found it. Then she charged up the stairs and began hacking at the cellar door.

Skip looked up the staircase to see that the entire second floor was ablaze. There was no way he would even make it up the stairs, which would surely be in flames soon. He heard an explosion from above and embers and pieces of ceiling splattered about him. He ran down the first-floor hallway checking in each room until he got to the kitchen.

It was when he was standing in the kitchen debating what to do next that he heard pounding. Coughing in the thickening smoke, he frantically searched for the source, finding it when he saw an axe make its way through the cellar door. Running over, he yelled, "Stop! I'm going to unlock the door." He grabbed a potholder off the counter and undid the lock and opened it, overjoyed to see Liliana standing there, axe in hand.

"We have to get out of here," he cried as an explosion hit behind them in the dining room. "Come on."

Liliana remained where she was. "My father is down there."

Skip pulled her up toward him. "Go out the back door. I'll get him." Then he hurtled down the stairs.

When another explosion rocked her father's office, Liliana did as Skip instructed and ran through the back door. She had just gotten outside, when, to her horror, another explosion hit the kitchen.

"No!" she cried. She started to go back in when arms enveloped her and a woman's voice said, "Liliana, you can't."

At the sound of the voice, Liliana's heart stuttered. "Mother?" she said, and then everything went dark.

28

Liliana heard voices and felt something placed over her mouth, then air filled her lungs. Opening her eyes, she saw a man adjusting an IV bag and her mother's face.

"It is really you," she mumbled underneath the oxygen mask.

"You're awake," said her mother, leaning forward and smiling.

When Liliana tried to speak again, her mother said, "Shh. Save your voice. You had quite an ordeal. They're going to take you to the hospital."

Suddenly, Liliana remembered Skip going back down for her father. She pulled the oxygen mask off and cried, "Skip and Father. Did they get out of the basement?"

Her mother frowned. "I don't think the firemen have found your father or anyone else."

At her mother's words, Liliana began shrieking and yanking at her IV. "We have to go get them!"

Her mother gripped Liliana's shoulders to stop her. "I'll tell the firemen. Please, lie back down and let the paramedic help you."

Liliana was eased back onto the gurney as her mother jumped out of the ambulance. He put the oxygen mask back on her face, and despite trying to remain awake, she soon found herself drifting off.

Liliana opened her eyes to the sight of her mother dozing in a chair next to her hospital bed. With the knowledge their reunion hadn't been a dream came tears of joy that flowed down her face onto the pillow.

Her sniffling soon woke her mother, who sat up and smiled. "You're awake." She put her hand on Liliana's.

Through hazy tears, Liliana sobbed, "I never thought I'd see you again."

Her mother reached for a tissue and dabbed Liliana's face to dry it. "I'm sorry. I know I have a lot of explaining to do, but first the good news. The firemen were able to get to your father and another man named Skip in the basement. Thank goodness you told me they were down there. It turns out there was a safe room in case of attack. Fireproof, but it wouldn't have been able to withstand the weight of the building for much longer."

As her mother's words sunk in, Liliana choked out, "Are they going to be okay?"

Her mother nodded vigorously. "Yes, they both are suffering from smoke inhalation like you. Your father has a bad burn on one arm, and Skip has a concussion, but otherwise, they're going to be just fine." She kissed Liliana's forehead. "And so are you."

Relief flooded through Liliana. Skip was alive, and her father. She clasped her mother's hands in hers and whispered, "Thank you."

"This Skip," her mother said softly. "He obviously means something to you. Is he from the commune?"

"No, he's from the outside. I met him when I escaped."

"You left?" Her mother looked surprised. "We have a lot of catching up to do. You must be thirsty. Let me give you some water."

Liliana took the paper cup her mother gave her and sucked down half of the water through a straw. When she finished, she said, "I want to see Skip. Can you take me to him?"

When Skip woke up in the hospital, the lights were low. For a moment, he struggled to remember what had happened; but then it all came flooding back. Though he had tried to get Liliana's father up the basement staircase, an explosion above made it clear they wouldn't be getting out. It was then that the man mentioned a safe room. Skip managed to get them in the shelter right before the floor from above collapsed. Once they were in the little room, which was no more than thirty-square-feet, he noticed that though it was stuffy, there seemed to be fresh air coming in from some-where. He took out his cellphone and flashed the light around to find a small vent to the outside.

"Whoever created this was a genius," he said. "As long as the structure is reinforced, we just might make it out of here alive."

Skip sat down next to the man. "I only know you as Liliana's father," he said. "What's your first name?"

"Shelton. You aren't really an unemployed mechanic, are you?"

"No."

"You came for my daughter."

"I did," said Skip.

"You must have met each other on the outside."

"It's a bit complicated but the short answer is yes."

The man sighed. "I thought when we came to the commune that it would be a good life for our family, but I was wrong. Liliana suffered. I see that now. Especially when her mother left."

Skip knew they should probably conserve their air, but he had to know—for Liliana. "What happened to her mother?"

"I truly don't know. The leadership told me she had agreed to their terms to leave Liliana behind and was living on the outside, but nothing more. I've tried over the last several years to find out, but I haven't been able to. And now to discover that Oliver is her son. None of it makes sense."

Just then, Skip heard voices calling his and Shelton's names. "We're in here," he began shouting, doing so until his voice became hoarse. For a time, it was quiet, and he feared they hadn't heard him. But then suddenly, it sounded like water was hammering the room, and before long a man yelled, "Step away from the door!"

When the door was busted open with pickaxes, two firemen swooped in to help them out and through the rubble of ashes and soggy burned wood. When they got outside, Skip looked around for Liliana, but didn't see her anywhere.

"There was a woman with long, auburn hair," he said to one of the firemen. "Did you see her?"

"Yes, she was taken to the hospital in an ambulance, which is where you're going now."

As the man said this, Skip felt dizzy. He put his hand to the back of his head and felt wetness. When his vision suddenly became spotty, he started to fall forward before the fireman grabbed ahold of him. "Head wound on this one," he heard him say.

A nurse walked into the hospital room then and smiled. "You're awake. That's a good sign." She checked the computer next to his bed. "It looks like you have a few stitches, and a concussion. Plus, smoke inhalation. How are you feeling?"

"Okay, except for a bad headache," he said. "The man who came in with me. Is he?"

"He has a severe burn on his arm, so they have him in the burn unit right now, but he should be fine."

"Has there been anyone to see me? A woman?" he asked.

"I've been with you since they checked you in several hours ago. No, you haven't had any visitors."

Skip lay back on the bed. "Okay, thank you."

The nurse put her hand on his shoulder. "I'm going to let the doctor know you're awake."

Skip closed his eyes and sighed. If he had been here several hours, why hadn't Liliana come to see him?

When there was a sound at the door, he opened his eyes hoping to see her, but it was the doctor.

"Glad to see you awake," said the physician, an older man with gray hair and sideburns. He shined a light into Skip's eyes and then checked the computer screen. "I understand that you're feeling okay except for a headache. I'm going to give you some pain reliever for that. You'll probably have a headache off and on for the next several days, and fatigue is very common."

"I'm a pilot," said Skip. "How long until it's safe for me to fly?"

"Let's take things one step at a time. I want to keep you here for observation for the rest of the night, and then we'll reevaluate tomorrow. Get some sleep. The more you rest, the quicker you'll heal."

Skip closed his eyes. The sooner he healed, the sooner he could get out of here and forget the last several days ever happened. The least Liliana could have done after he'd risked his life to save her and her father was come visit him. But then they hadn't made each other any promises.

29

When Skip opened his eyes, he saw a woman looking out the window of his hospital room, her back to him.

"Hello?"

His visitor turned around to face him. She looked to be in her fifties and wore slacks and a blue blouse. Her chestnut brown hair fell in soft waves to her shoulders, and her eyes, a warm hazel, sparkled when she said, "You're awake."

"Do I know you?"

The woman smiled. "We haven't yet had the pleasure."

Just then the bathroom door opened and out walked Liliana. When she saw Skip, she rushed to his side. "I thought you'd never wake up! How are you feeling? The doctor said you have a concussion."

Skip looked to the woman and back to Liliana. "Is this your mother?"

Liliana laughed. "I guess there is a resemblance. Skip, this is Jill. And this," she beamed at her mother, "is Skip."

"Liliana has told me all about you," said Jill.

"She has?"

"Oh, yes, you're all she's been talking about. I know you're a pilot, and that you grew up on a farm in North Dakota." She glanced at Liliana, whose face had flushed. "Let me step out of the room so you can catch up before I say anything else to embarrass her."

When the door closed, Skip said, "I thought you left me."

Liliana frowned. "I'm sorry you thought that. I'm so sorry for so many things. When I got out of the house and the kitchen exploded, I tried to go back in for you, but my mother showed up and stopped me. The paramedics treated me for smoke inhalation, and when I asked about you and Father, I was told that no one else made it out alive." Anguish filled her face. "In my hysteria, I apparently got it across to my mother that you and my father were in the basement, so she told the firemen, and they pulled you out just in time."

"How long have I been out?"

"The nurse said you woke up last night about eight, and now it's noon the following day."

"You said you're sorry about so many things. What did you mean by that?"

Liliana scooted her chair closer to the bed. "I'm sorry I got you involved in all of this and that you could have been killed. But mostly, I'm sorry..." Skip waited as Liliana stopped, her voice heavy with emotion. She put her hand on his chest. "I'm sorry that I didn't tell you I loved you when we made love." Her eyes filled with tears as she choked out, "I do love you, Skip. With all my heart."

"Say it again," said Skip, who thought he had never heard sweeter words.

Liliana laughed. "I love you, Skip Moore. I love you. I love you. I love you. And you'll never stop me from saying it."

The doctor kept Skip in the hospital under observation for two more days. During that time, Liliana and her mother spent a great deal of time in his room making sure he was ultra-comfortable and that he had all the takeout he could eat.

While Skip was recovering, they also had time to catch up. The conversation was strained at first.

"I am so sorry for what happened," said Jill when they sat down in the hospital cafeteria with coffee and donuts the first day. "I can only say that the wrong people persuaded me at the right time. When we originally moved to the commune, I was hoodwinked like all the converts. I truly believed that our decision to live there was a good one. That you would thrive in a community free of crime and the evil ways of society. But within a year of living there, I began to see what was really going on. That the cult controlled everyone, and that once people came in, they weren't allowed to leave, even if they were miserable. For whatever reason, your father remained loyal to the cause. I guess in many ways it gave him a sense of purpose. He loved the order and rules and regulations. I think they made him, as they made many of the members, feel safe. But the system was choking the life out of me."

Her mother stopped and tore off a piece of glazed donut and held it up. "Even the simplest pleasures were forbidden." She put the donut in her mouth and chewed, then washed it down with a sip of coffee. "When I asked your father to leave, he became very angry and told me it was forbidden and reminded me of the contract we signed when we arrived. A contract that unfortunately I didn't read very well."

"What did the contract say?" asked Liliana.

"That we agreed to remain in perpetuity in exchange for the cult taking us in. And it stipulated that if a member wishes to leave, they must go before the leadership and explain their reasons, which I did." Her mother looked at Liliana, her eyes shiny with unspent tears.

"Let me guess, they refused your request," said Liliana.

Her mother nodded. "Your father was not allowed at the meeting—or should I say sentencing. When I protested against their ruling, they voted me a heretic and removed me immediately, taking me to another facility where they brainwash members into seeing the error of their ways and embracing the cult. In retrospect, I can see that they didn't want former cult members out in public telling the truth."

She stopped and pushed her hair over her shoulders. "The psychological abuse I endured at the other facility included them convincing me that you were better off at the commune. They even showed me photos of you and your father. You looked happy."

"I was far from happy," said Liliana, brushing away angry tears. "What I needed was a mother."

Jill took a deep breath. "I realize that now, and I'm truly, truly sorry. If I could take back those years, I would. Though they tried to reprogram me, and I became a confused and broken woman in the process, at the back of my mind, I knew there was a better way to live. So, one night I escaped." Her expression became pained. "Even when I made it to the outside, though, I had to work through the toxic, destructive programming before I could function in the world. When I did, it was then that I began planning to break into the compound and get you out. There are people who help, but their fees are steep. Finally, not too long ago I had the money, but when it was time to go in, my contact couldn't locate you."

"That must have been when I escaped," said Liliana.

"How did you get out?"

"I got in the grocer's truck after a delivery," said Liliana, who took a sip of coffee. "How did you end up at the commune the day of the fire? And how does Oliver fit in?"

"When I was held in the other compound, there was a

man who managed to get into my psyche, and my bed. I became pregnant with Oliver." She ran her hands through her hair. "I couldn't imagine raising him when I had abandoned you, so I gave him up through the cult's adoptive program. When I was working on getting in to extract you, I discovered Oliver was working with your father, and I was afraid that he would tell him, and you, who he was. I wanted to be the one to explain it. The morning of the fire, the company I hired to infiltrate called to tell me that the compound's infrastructure was failing, and it would be a good time to breach. When we went in and I saw the house burning, I could only think that you might be in there, and it turns out you were. I realize that you may never forgive me for any of this, and I've accepted that fact."

After her mother finished speaking, Liliana stared at the table for a time. Finally, she spoke. "It sounds like you suffered a great deal."

"The most suffering I did was knowing that I had abandoned you."

While Liliana had felt anger and dismay for so many years, all she could think of at that very moment was how glad she was to be with her mother now. "I can't promise I won't be angry with you sometimes, but I'm ready to work on forgiving you for what happened," Liliana told her. "I understand the cult's manipulative tactics quite well."

Her mother smiled and took Liliana's hands in hers. "You can't know how wonderful it is to hear you say that. I promise I'll work the rest of my life to make up for my absence."

"What about Father?" asked Liliana. "Have you seen him?"

Her mother shook her head. "Not yet. They don't allow visitors in the burn unit. And to be honest, I'm not quite ready. Have you heard from the FBI if he will be charged once he's released from the hospital?"

Liliana had gotten an update from Agent Leonardo earlier that day. "The computer records showed that Father is not culpable for the arms smuggling. As he said, he stopped the activity when he took over, and it was the reason Geoffrey was ousted. He truly was trying to run a misguided utopia."

"And Oliver?" asked her mother quietly.

"Oliver and Georgina were captured at the Canadian border. It turns out they were working with the militant group to supply them with arms, which is why they were trying to get rid of me and Father. When the group pulled out just recently, Oliver decided to burn down the place and run. He's now being held for terrorism, gun smuggling, and arson. The FBI is also interrogating other members who they suspect of wrongdoing, and then offering the rest of the residents trauma counseling, as well as reuniting children with their parents."

"For those who take advantage of the counseling, it will take time, but there is life after the cult. I'm living proof," said her mother.

"You mean we're living proof," corrected Liliana.

"Enough talk of the past. Tell me your future plans. Do they include Skip?"

Liliana smiled. "Skip has asked me to fly out with him to North Dakota when he's released to attend to something important. I know you and I are just catching up, but I told him I would go."

Her mother squeezed Liliana's hands. "Skip is crazy about you, and he's a good man. Solid and strong, and not easily swayed. You go with him. I'll be right here. I'm not going anywhere. I promise."

30

By the second day in the hospital, Skip was feeling more clearheaded, so he decided to check his voicemail. When he turned on his phone, he was surprised to see several calls from North Dakota.

He dialed River's number, and she answered almost immediately. "Skip, thank goodness I got you. I know you said you had something to attend to, but things have become time sensitive. We must produce proof that the land belongs to the tribe by the end of the week, as the area is scheduled to become a federal nature preserve. I know it's probably a long shot, but I thought I'd let you know."

"I think I have the proof you're looking for," he said.

"You do?" said River, her voice becoming excited. "Could you get it here before the end of the week?"

Skip considered logistics. "The proof is in Acapulco in my apartment, but I'm in Washington state in the hospital. I'm being released tomorrow. I have an idea, though. Let me make a phone call and get back to you."

Skip hung up and called Carlos.

"Please tell me you survived your recent adventure," said his friend when he answered.

"Kind of. I'm in the hospital, and I need your help."

"I'm no doctor, *amigo.*"

"That's not the kind of help I need. Can you go to my apartment in Acapulco and get some documents and bring them here to me?"

"Where the hell is here?"

"Washington state."

"Whoa, hold on. You want me to fly all the way to Mexico from Florida and then up to Washington? And I suppose you want me to do this *pronto?*"

"*Ahora*, yes," said Skip. "I can arrange for private flights."

"This have anything to do with the *chica?*"

"It has to do with my mother."

"Say no more. I'll do it."

When Skip was released from the hospital the following morning, he and Liliana picked up their things at the motel, then returned the rental car at the airport and prepared the plane for the flight to North Dakota while they awaited Carlos's arrival.

It was late morning when Carlos landed. Skip and Liliana went to greet him as he got off the plane.

"Skip, *amigo,*" said Carlos, who despite flying for nearly twenty-four hours, looked wide awake and refreshed. He handed him an envelope.

"Thanks so much for this," said Skip. "You remember Liliana."

Carlos nodded at her. "Hard to forget."

"You're going to need to wait until tomorrow for your flight out," said Skip. "I hope that's not a problem. My buddy has to do a run to Northern Canada, but he'll be back for you in the morning."

Carlos slid his hands into his jeans pockets. "I can hang here for a while. Although it's kind of chilly compared to Sarasota in May."

"I've got a great idea," said Skip. "You can catch up with Esmerelda. She lives not too far from here."

At the guarded look that washed over Carlos's face, Skip backtracked. "Hey, it was just a suggestion."

The flight from Washington to North Dakota went smoothly. They landed in the late afternoon and went into the airport terminal to meet River.

"Skip, it's so nice to finally meet you," she said, giving him a warm smile and reaching out to shake his hand. She was tall and slender, her posture graceful and confident, her long, jet-black hair flowing straight down her back.

"It's a pleasure to meet you, as well," said Skip. "River, this is Liliana. Liliana, River."

"So nice to meet you, Liliana," said River. "We are so grateful to Skip for bringing the proof we need to regain what is rightfully ours."

"Let's hope it's what you need," said Skip, handing her the envelope.

River opened the clasp and pulled out the map, her face becoming animated. Then she removed the paper and read it, her lips moving slightly as she did so. When she finished, she beamed at Skip. "From what I can tell, this is what we've been looking for. Thanks to your mother, we will be able to preserve the land for our people."

"I'm sorry it took me so long to get it to you," said Skip.

"We have it now. That's all that matters. I need to get

these documents to the council, but did you want to see the land before you go?"

"I would, yes," said Skip.

"Great, I'll take you there now. It's not far."

They climbed into River's Jeep and headed out onto the highway. Soon, they passed familiar fields of oats, and Skip inhaled deeply.

"Has it been a while since you've been home?" asked River.

"Too long," said Skip.

A few miles later, River slowed and drove down a dirt road, coming to a stop at a bluff overlooking prairie land. They all got out of the car and walked to the edge. Below lay dry brush land pockmarked by occasional splashes of green. A crow flew overhead, its cawing echoing in the still air.

"It is only a little more than a square mile, but this piece of land is of ecological significance," said River. "The land happens to have an abundance of Western Prairie Fringed Orchid growing. It's an endangered species. And now our tribe will regain ownership of the land and its natural beauty."

"My mother loved gardening and especially flowers," said Skip as he gazed out at the land set against bright-blue, cloudless sky. "She used to say, 'To touch the earth is to have harmony with nature.'"

"An old Sioux proverb. Excuse me for a minute," she said. "I'm going to let the council know we'll be there soon."

After she walked out of earshot, Liliana said, "You're at home here. I feel it."

Skip took a deep breath. "I fled North Dakota fifteen years ago to get away from the painful memory of the loss of my mother, but you're right, I am home here."

"And Mexico?" asked Liliana.

"I think it's time to come home."

"What will you do?"

"I've always wanted to run a flight school."

"You would be great at that," said Liliana.

Skip turned to her and took her hands in his. "Would you leave your home in Washington and come live here with me?" His heart seemed to stop as he waited for her answer.

Liliana smiled. "My home is with you."

EPILOGUE

Liliana's and Skip's stories are complete, but Carlos Rincon's is just beginning....

Carlos watched Skip's plane take off from the airport terminal, his friend's suggestion echoing in his mind. Could he, or better yet, should he, reach out to Esmerelda while he was here in Washington? He pulled out his phone and went to his contacts, then stared at her number. Would she even answer after the way he had left things?

"Fuck it," he said to himself, then pressed her number. It rang several times before she answered.

"Carlos?"

"It's me, *hermosa*."

"Why are you calling me?"

"I happen to be in Washington for the day and night." Carlos paused. "I thought maybe I could see you."

Silence on the other end of the line.

"You still there, *hermosa?*"

"Don't call me *hermosa*. You lost that right."

Carlos sighed. "About what happened, I was hoping we could talk."

"Now? You want to talk about it now, five years later?"

"Yes, I do."

More silence, then finally she said, "Okay. I'll give you five minutes to explain yourself. Meet me at—."

Suddenly, Carlos heard what sounded like struggling, and then Esmerelda cried out, "What do you want? Let go of me!" right before the line went dead.

See what happens with Carlos and Esmerelda in *Discovered Cover-up.*

A NOTE FOR YOU

Dear Reading Gem,

Thanks for spending time with me, Liliana and Skip! While each of the books in the Discovered Truth Series can be read as a standalone, it's fun to experience the progression and get to know the characters. The series progresses as minor characters introduced in each book become main characters in subsequent books. It's exciting to see what they'll do next!

The Discovered Truth series features complex, gutsy women and equally complicated, charismatic men who find themselves immersed in dangerous and intriguing modern-day challenges, such as human trafficking, drug smuggling, organ theft, national security threats, and identity theft. When the heroine and hero meet, worlds collide and sparks fly, kindling unforgettable romance and intrigue.

Thanks again and talk soon!

STAY ENLIGHTENED

Dear Reading Gem, thanks for reading! Let's stay in touch.

Join my weekly newsletter Julie's Reading Gems here. You get a free prequel novella to the series for signing up. There are also weekly giveaways and contests to win free books in the series.

You can also find me on my website at https://www.juliebawdendavis.com/fiction/fiction-books/the-discovered-truth-series/, email me at Julie@JulieBawdenDavis.com, and follow me on Amazon.

Escape to Unforgettable Romance and Intrigue...

YOUR OPINION MATTERS

If you liked this book, please leave a review on Amazon, GoodReads, BookBub, or all three. If you don't wish to leave a review or don't have time, please leave a rating. Every star helps!

BOOKS IN THE DISCOVERED TRUTH SERIES

Discovered Beginnings:
(FREE at https://www.juliebawdendavis.com/fiction)
Discovered Secrets
Discovered Memories
Discovered Indiscretions
Discovered Liaisons
Discovered Betrayal
Discovered Denial
Discovered Distractions
Discovered Deception
Discovered Lies
Discovered Vengeance
Discovered Redemption
Discovered Obsession
Discovered Transgressions
Discovered Suspicion
Discovered Escape
Discovered Promises
Discovered Cover-up
Discovered Intentions

Box Sets

The Discovered Truth Series Box Set Books 1-4

The Discovered Truth Series Box Set Books 5-8

The Discovered Truth Series Box Set Books 9-12

The Discovered Truth Series Box Set Books 13-16

www.ingramcontent.com/pod-product-compliance
Lightning Source LLC
Chambersburg PA
CBHW030349200626
46808CB00022B/825